CHARM ARTIST

SIGNS OF LIFE SERIES
BOOK 4

CRESTON MAPES

STAND-ALONE THRILLERS
I Am In Here

Nobody

SIGNS OF LIFE SERIES
Signs of Life

Let My Daughter Go

I Pick You

Charm Artist

Son & Shield

Secrets in Shadows

THE CRITTENDON FILES
Fear Has a Name

Poison Town

Sky Zone

ROCK STAR CHRONICLES
Dark Star: Confessions of a Rock Idol

Full Tilt

PRAISE FOR *CHARM ARTIST*

"I was hooked on the first page of Creston Mapes' new book, Charm Artist. I could not put it down and I had to find out what was going to happen next. Just like n his other books in the Signs of Life Series, Creston's character, Detective Wayne Deetz, did not fail to solve the crime, even though he was on vacation! My surprise was the role his wife, Joanie, played in helping solve the crime. This is a fast-paced, enjoyable read." — **Gail Mundy**

"There's a reason Creston Mapes is an Amazon #1 Best-selling author; he's an absolute genius when it comes to writing suspense. In this new installment of *Signs of* Life series, Detective Wayne Deetz and his wife Joanie are on a well-deserved vacation in Sedona, Arizona. But Deetz quickly finds himself pulling back the curtain on the dark and seedy world of opioid addiction in all its ugliest glory. So much for a quiet vacation with the wife … Once again Mapes takes us on a wild ride, and leaves us breathless to the very last page." — **Best-selling Author Diane Moody**

"If you like suspense, Creston Mapes will not disappoint. This fourth book in the *Signs of Life* series has Detective Wayne Deetz and wife Joanie on vacation visiting her best friend, Suzanne. The detective can't ignore suspicious behavior of Suzanne and her boyfriend, especially when they learn of her lies about leaving town. Even though Deetz is supposed to be considering retirement, police work is in his blood. He can't just walk away from the danger Suzanne is in. You don't have to read the books in order, but you will want to read everything Creston Mapes writes. Ginger Aster, faithful fan." — **Ginger Astor**

"I was captivated from the first chapter. I think *Charm Artist* is the best of the four in the series so far. Honestly, I couldn't put it down, and read it in just two days. Once again, Creston Mapes writes straight out of the major headlines and gives us a 'can't put it down' thriller." — **Missy Caulk**

This is a work of fiction. Names, characters, organizations, places, events, and incidents are either products of the author's imagination or are used fictitiously. Any resemblance to actual persons, living or dead, or actual events is purely coincidental.

No part of this book may be reproduced or stored in a retrieval system, or transmitted in any form or by any means, electronic, mechanical, photocopying, recording, or otherwise, without express written permission of the publisher.

Copyright © 2021 Creston Mapes, Inc
Published by Rooftop Press

*Huge shout out to Hannah Mapes for insights on
opioids, methadone, and the world of pain killer addiction.*

*Gratitude to Lt. Lucas Wilcoxson of the Sedona Police Department for
insights about police uniforms, cars, patrols, and procedures.*

The Mayo Clinic proved an excellent source of information—thank you.

Bernard Mapes, thanks for helping me with the business-side of book writing.

*Grateful to Ken Fite, Jason Chatraw, Erik Carter, Ken Moody, and Jonathan
Cullen for sharing knowledge and insights on the exciting world of Indie
publishing.*

*Patty—thanks for your time, effort, and editing prowess. For someone who
doesn't like suspense, you did a bang-up job.*

*Shout out to my amazing early reader team: Diane Moody, Ginger Aster,
Missy Caulk, Gail Mundy, and Rachel Savage. You have each supported my
work from day one and I'm grateful for your enthusiasm.*

*Drew Bott, thank you for the wonderful job you've done
narrating this and each audio book in the Signs of Life Series!*

1

It both bothered Octavius and aroused him that Wayne and Joanie Deetz had shown up unexpectedly in Sedona, Arizona, for what they were calling a two-week get away from their lives in Portland, Oregon. (How anyone could live in that dank, woodsy, Godforsaken rain forest, Octavius would never know.)

He stepped back from the large canvas in his size twelve, soft leather OluKai boots, tilted his bald head, and examined the current masterpiece—a huge commissioned abstract watercolor painting for the living room of the mayor of Jessup, Marsden Maddox. 'Mars' and his regal, much younger wife, Candace, had become dear friends of his over the past few years; *partners in crime, you could aptly call them.* Octavius sniggered.

He walked to the vast windows of his studio, which was nestled in the cliffside city of Jessup, a mysterious old copper mining town just outside of Sedona that had boomed in the 1800s. He touched the cold window with the back of his big hand and shivered from the December chill; he did not like the cold and longed for the Arizona heat of summer. He reached for his shiny silver insulated canister and stuffed his pipe with tobacco. When he couldn't find his lighter, he crossed to his welding torch, snapped it on and fired up the pipe, puffing and blowing until the brown shreds glowed hot orange.

He went back to the window and peered across the dry valley at the mysterious looking old hotel on the side of Valentine Mountain which had once been known as the Sanctuary Hills Psychiatric Institution. It had torn black awnings, overgrown trees and bushes, and was still open for business. A number of ancient, clapboard hotels still dotted the side of the mountain, most of them having once served as rousing bordellos during the city's heyday. Everything from impressive, sleek mansions carved into the side of the mountain to dilapidated shotgun shacks on stilts filled the hillside town. It was even rumored that ghosts converged on Jessup back in the day—and still haunted many of the buildings in town.

That was why 'Octavius' had been the perfect name he'd chosen when he'd relocated to Arizona several years earlier from St. Augustine, Florida. According to history, the 'Octavius' had been a legendary ghost ship from the 18th century which was found shipwrecked by a scouting party that discovered the entire crew of twenty-eight people below deck, frozen, and almost perfectly preserved. The captain's body was said to be sitting upright at a table, with pen in hand and the captain's log in front of him. The bodies of a woman and child, covered in blankets, were found in his quarters.

Octavius shivered again, crossed to the thermostat, and inched it up till he heard the furnace kick on. He eyed the large studio, with its glossy wood floor and his many unique and masterful paintings and sculptures displayed precisely all around the border. He was proud of the studio and the reputation he'd built in such a short time. In fact, why not toast himself? It was 3 p.m. and happy hour somewhere.

Pipe in mouth, he reached behind his back with both hands, untied, tightened, and re-tied his brown canvas apron as he walked into the adjoining office. It smelled of incense and was pleasantly furnished with two comfy gray leather chairs, plush oval rug, high-end Bluetooth stereo system, enormous desktop Mac, large wine refrigerator with glass door and numerous shelves, and abstract photographs all over the walls. The photographs were mostly of women in seductive garb—and mystic rock formations from in and around Sedona.

He grabbed the stereo remote, clicked on one of his favorite playlists, and the studio filled up with rich bass and the mesmerizing New Age sound of flutes, harps, and melodic piano. Octavius was indeed proud. He set his broad shoulders back, went to the bar, dropped five coffee beans in a drink glass one by one, poured two fingers of Sambuca, and took a slow sip. *Ahh.* He savored the anise-flavored liqueur with its notes of elderflower and licorice. Thirty-eight percent alcohol by volume—a fine way to get the old creative juices flowing.

He puffed and puffed, but the pipe had gone out. He cursed, went over to a copper junk dish on his desk, grabbed a small torch lighter, and fired up the bowl again.

Laughter erupted in the hallway beyond his studio. Octavius took his drink and pipe, walked quietly across the wood floor of the studio to the far door, and leaned out. It was a bunch of roly-poly women in red and green, hosting a tacky Christmas thrift sale to raise funds for some kid with cancer. He wished they wouldn't do such things on the approach to his studio, but he didn't have much say over what they did beyond his doors.

He certainly couldn't complain. The old high school had served as the perfect headquarters for his studio. And Jessup was the ideal locale for it, because of the town's artsy, hip, eclectic vibe—something he'd discovered early on that the wealthy, trinket-filled tourist town of Sedona did not offer. Jessup was a modern-day artist colony and Octavius had built quite the reputation there, teaching painting classes and selling his works like hotcakes—both to the locals and to wide-eyed tourists from Sedona, Prescott, Flagstaff, the Metro Phoenix area, and beyond.

He blew a stream of smoke into the hallway, smirked at a heavy woman wearing a Santa hat, walked back into the studio, and studied the painting again. It was getting there, but still needed *something*. Little did his clients know he hid secrets in the paintings—hints from the past, clues about the future. Speaking of the future, it was maddeningly bothersome this Deetz couple had arrived at the doorstep of Octavius's home in Sedona, because the husband Deetz was, of all things, a cop. *Very poor timing, indeed.*

But really, Octavius had to snicker. This Wayne Deetz character was old as the hills and on the cusp of retirement. He was balding, graying, and wore enormous smudged glasses from the Seventies; he could certainly be no threat.

The Deetz's arrival could actually add some fun to the calendar. Deetz had said the main reason they'd come to Arizona was to think and "pray" about their future (the prayer part made Octavius chuckle to no end.) Deetz was a year away from retirement but, due to some recent hullabaloo at his work in Portland, which involved quite a wallop of a concussion, he was considering cashing in his chips early. The trip was designed to help them clear their heads and come to a decision about their future.

If they want real spiritual enlightenment they need to explore the vortices at Boynton Canyon or Bell Rock.

Speaking of hidden energy, Deetz's wife Joanie was the exhilarating half of the equation. With her short cropped brown hair and hints of gray, she made Octavius's blood course through his veins like a frenzied teenager. She was Deetz's age, about sixty, but had the petite, firm body of a thirty-five-year-old fitness instructor. Octavius was quite sure that beneath her classy, conservative exterior, Joanie was one hot package. The thought of her gave him shivers.

Joanie Deetz was a lifelong friend of Octavius's most recent partner, Suzanne Bartholomew. The two women had rekindled their childhood friendship several weeks earlier and, somehow, Suzanne had forgotten to mention to Octavius that the Deetzes were renting an Airbnb over in Red Rock City, another of the manufactured towns popping up around Sedona like cardboard greeting cards. The Deetz's timing could be problematic, but Octavius got his thrills living on the edge.

With the memory of Joanie's alluring smile, full dark eyebrows, and robust figure lingering in his mind, Octavius grabbed the plastic bottle of water from his carousel and sprayed the upper right corner of the painting. The indigo had dried too dark; he let it run a bit and dappled it with a sponge. *Better.*

It was happening again.

That frightening . . . exhilarating *pull.*

You should stop thinking about this, about her.

But, as with the others, he just couldn't get Joanie off his mind.

She was a magnet—just like the mysterious cosmic forces of the red rocks.

He sipped the Sambuca, swirled the liqueur in his mouth, and basked in the slight burn as it went down.

The darn pipe had gone out again.

Oh well.

He tossed it in the big ashtray next to his carousel, excited by the notion he would be seeing Joanie again that evening.

Much to do before then, including checking on Suzanne.

He eyed the painting and found the small letters he'd blended into the side of a triangle he'd created with a mixture of cadmium red and burnt sienna.

A bit too obvious.

He smiled, snatched a mop brush, plopped it in and out of water, dabbed it in the burnt sienna, and swished it over the hidden lettering, just enough so the letters J-O-A-N-I-E couldn't be too readily spotted by the casual observer.

2

Wayne Deetz walked into the kitchen of the Airbnb tiny house, tucked in the foothills of Red Rock City, Arizona, cleaning his glasses with the front flap of his flannel shirt. Joanie was pouring a cup of hot tea.

"Talked to the kids," he said. "All's fine, believe it or not."

"Thanks for checking on them," Joanie said.

"Brandon said you got a box from eBay."

"Oh, finally. That's the bird feeder I ordered."

"J.P. and Tammy haven't been over yet," he said.

"Well, it's only been a few days. I'm sure they'll get over soon. Why? Is everything okay?"

"Yeah. They both seemed fine."

"Is he getting her to play practice?"

"Yeah. Leena said he's been great. Picks her up right on time. Amazing."

"That is amazing," Joanie said. "Want tea?"

"What kind?"

"Green or peppermint."

"Sure, I'll try peppermint. What the heck. Gotta branch out. Between the nature hikes and the bike rides and the tea, I'm becoming a new man."

"I feel like I'm just starting to relax. It's taken what, three days?" Joanie said.

"I know what you mean. I'm not there yet, but I'm getting there. That bed is amazing."

"How's your head?"

"Good." Deetz fibbed slightly. He still didn't feel completely like himself since getting his skull bashed in at the Sunny Carlisle-Blaine Milligan home invasion weeks earlier, but he didn't want to think about that, or any police work.

He and Joanie had come to Arizona to clear their heads and decide next steps. Deetz had a year to go until he received his full retirement benefits package for thirty-five years of service with the Portland PD. But after he had worked, and they had endured, the Portland massacre of 2019 and copycat attempt a year later, daughter Leena's kidnapping, then the home invasion involving an acquaintance of their close friends, Tyson Cooper and Callie Freeland, they were considering having Deetz turn in his badge early and take the reduced benefits package.

His boss, Sergeant Dolby Tidwell, had insisted he take several weeks off to recover completely from the concussion, and make up his mind whether he wanted to return for his last year or not.

Son Brandon, 22, was home from college on winter break and was watching daughter Leena, 18, who had autism. Son J.P., 24, and his girlfriend Tammy were supposed to check in at the house now and then, and even spend a night or two while Wayne and Joanie were in Arizona.

Joanie brought Deetz a cup of steaming tea. "Lean down. Let me see your head," she said.

He took the cup and bent over so she could see the scar where Milligan had cracked him with a gun.

"It looks really good, honey," Joanie said. "The swelling's almost all gone."

"Is there a scar?"

"You've asked me that a hundred times. Of course. You had twelve stitches. But no one can see it. It's at the very top of your head."

"All my flowing hair covers it up?"

Joanie laughed.

His balding had been the brunt of an ongoing joke for several years.

"How'd Suzanne seem to you?" Joanie took her tea into the living room and sat on the leather couch with her legs folded up under her. They had a beautiful view of Sedona's Red Rock Mountains out the sliding glass doors.

Deetz shrugged. "Okay, I guess. Thinner than I remember. I mean, I don't know her like you do. Why?"

"She didn't seem like herself. She's always so upbeat and full of life. She was kind of . . . blah. It was like she was in la-la land, like she wasn't even really there. She said she was just tired because she stayed up really late the night before."

"Well, we were only with them for a few minutes."

"Yeah."

"Maybe life with old Octavius isn't all it's cracked up to be." Deetz chuckled.

"He's something, isn't he?" she said.

Deetz raised his eyebrows and smirked. "He definitely seems to be the man about town—or at least wants to be."

"She was also scratching a lot. Didn't you notice?" Joanie said.

"I didn't. Probably because Octavius was keeping my attention with all his self-praise."

"He's not someone I would ever imagine Suzanne would date. My gosh, not in the slightest," Joanie said. "He's got to be ten years younger than her."

"More than that!" Deetz sipped his tea, walked to the glass doors, and looked out at the burnt orange landscape. "He sure was interested in you."

Joanie chortled. "What's that supposed to mean?"

"He was obviously flirting with you." He glanced over his shoulder at her and smiled. Inside, he was slightly jealous, simply because Octavius was not only tall, handsome, and younger, but he was an artist and connoisseur of what seemed like—everything.

Joanie laughed. "I love it when you get jealous."

"He did come on strong. Don't you agree?"

"I mean, he was . . . inquisitive."

"He couldn't have gotten any closer to you."

She laughed. "He did invade my personal space. It was quite uncomfortable, actually."

"You didn't seem too upset by all the attention."

"Oh, Wayne, come on! Don't be like that. You saw how I kept inviting Suzanne back into the conversation—and you."

"Suzanne seemed used to his behavior."

Joanie said nothing.

"I hope he doesn't try to corner you again tonight," Deetz said.

"Wayne, what's wrong with you? You're never jealous. Come here."

He turned and faced her, but didn't go over. "Sorry hon. I didn't mean anything. He was just obviously attracted to you."

She shook her head and actually blushed. "I don't know what to say, honey. I didn't do anything to bring it on."

"I know you didn't." He turned and looked outside again. "I'm sorry I brought it up. It's stupid of me." He felt like an idiot and wished he hadn't said anything. It made him look weak and pitiful.

She didn't say anything.

He turned back around and headed for the kitchen, then stopped and reached out his hand for her cup. "You want me to top that off?"

She took his hand. "You're my main squeeze, Wayne Francis Deetz." She smiled and, when she saw his smile, she laughed. "Sure, I'll take more. Top me off, buddy."

He took both mugs to the kitchen and turned on the burner where the tea kettle sat. "What time are we due there tonight?" he asked.

"Cocktails at five, just in time to watch the sunset. Suzanne said it's quite a sight from his back deck."

"Splendid," Deetz said, sarcastically.

"Octavius will have the fire pit going and the heat lamps on."

He looked over and Joanie was holding her book up to her face, peering over the top at him with mischievous eyes. She lowered the book to reveal a huge grin.

They both shook their heads and laughed.

3

The streets of Sedona—decorated for Christmas with wreaths and strings of lights—were bumper-to-bumper with cars, pickups, and SUVs, and the sidewalks were packed with people carrying shopping bags and wandering endlessly. It was about fifty degrees approaching dusk, and the backdrop of the mountains—a combination of stark sun and black shade on orange rock—was stunning.

Joanie, in the passenger seat, worked the car's GPS like an air traffic control expert. "Let's not go the way it's saying. If you go straight another half-mile and turn left on Canyon Cove, that'll take us right up to his neighborhood," Joanie said.

"You sure?" Deetz said.

"Yeah, the way it wants to take us will have us zig-zagging on backroads all the way up there. Trust me."

"Okay." Deetz patiently steered the rental SUV through stop light after stop light, allowing masses of tourists to cross at each one.

Joanie reflected on the discussion with Wayne earlier that afternoon. She was surprised he was jealous of Octavius, because when they'd been at his house the first time, even though briefly, Wayne had shown no signs he was upset. He rarely got jealous. She wondered if he was feeling his age; she knew she did. Afterall, they were both in their sixties now, which was uncharted territory.

She thanked God they had each other. They truly were best friends.

Joanie admitted that Octavius had come on strong—and close. He was quite . . . was 'overpowering' the word? From his tall stature to his expensive clothes and cologne, to what appeared to be capped, almost neon white teeth—he was a charmer.

"Making a left on Canyon Cove, dear," Deetz said as he made the turn.

They made their way up to the dense, high-end neighborhood, in which the sleek, single-level homes sat at unique angles, seemingly carved right out of red rock canyons. Along the freshly blacktopped lanes, the houses were built with earthy brick and stone colors, rich wood stains, glass, and landscapes comprised of rocks, boulders, brush, and cacti—no lawns to mow. Many were decorated for the holidays.

"This is *really* nice," Joanie said. "How much do you think these go for?"

"Have to be at least a couple million," Deetz said. "Maybe more. Not sure."

They swung into Octavius's wide circular driveway and parked on the brown cobblestone. They got out. One of the bays in the three-car garage was open, revealing a silver Mercedes G-Class SUV, the kind that looked like a Jeep.

"I know those Benzes go for about two hundred grand," Deetz said as they approached the huge brown metal front doors with stained glass windows. Behind a horizontal smoked glass window over the front doors hung an enormous chandelier that was contemporary, not formal. No Christmas decorations in sight.

Joanie rang the doorbell. "I don't see Suzanne's car."

"Maybe she Ubered."

After a pause, one of the massive front doors lurched open. The sound of rich flutes and horns flowed out as Octavius filled the doorframe wearing a denim button down shirt, silver necklace with a thick silver-bar pendant, gold corduroy pants, and worn brown leather shoes. "Ah, the Deetzes. What a pleasure. So glad to have you. Come in, come in."

As he ushered them in with an outstretched arm, Joanie noticed again his huge, hairy hands. He looked Greek with his tan bald head, short goatee, and five o'clock shadow. His breath smelled of alcohol and his cologne was heavy, but very nice.

"Oh, my goodness, what smells so amazing?" Joanie said.

"Spicy basil shrimp." Octavius led them down the red tile hallway with mirrors on the walls, to the enormous living room with floor-to-ceiling picture windows. "I hope you like Thai food. Do you?"

"Oh, sure," Deetz said, glancing at Joanie.

"Oh, yes," Joanie said, raising her eyebrows at Wayne, because they never ate Thai food.

"Are you spicy people?" Octavius said. "Joanie, I know you must like it spicy." His seductive smile seemed to sparkle as he winked at her with brown marble eyes.

"Not too spicy, no," she said, avoiding Wayne's glance, because she was embarrassed by the spicy comment.

"Me either," Deetz said. "Mild for me, if you can swing it."

Octavius put his head back and laughed heartily. His neck was thick, and he was built like a rock. Joanie assumed he worked out often. He had a thick scar on the top of his head about two inches long. "No worries, my friends. I made some spicy and some mild. Suzanne likes it mild and I like it hot—the spicier the better. It's the Greek in me."

Joanie looked all around for Suzanne.

Octavius crossed to a wide fireplace on an enormous brick wall, flipped a switch, and flames jumped to life. "I'm afraid Suzanne is running late. What can I get you to drink? Cocktail? Wine? Perrier? Craft beer? We have several local craft breweries that hold their own."

Joanie looked at Wayne, then back at Octavius.

Before she could say Perrier, Octavius wheeled around presenting a bottle of white wine. "May I suggest a very nice Pinot Blanc? Grapes from Burgundy, France. Resembles a chardonnay. Oaked and full-bodied. Pairs ideally with our entree." His dark eyes burned into Joanie almost taking her breath away.

She nodded and smiled and felt herself blush. "Just what I was thinking."

Wayne smiled and nodded. "Sure. Sounds good." He rolled his eyes at Joanie.

"Now, the rule here at StoneSpell is that I serve the first round and you help yourself the rest of the evening. Sound good?" He opened the bottle in a flash, splashed the wine into three enormous glasses, and held his up. "A toast to the Deetzes and to your time here in the land of the red rocks. May you find direction, rejuvenation, and energy here in the mystic mountains."

His eyes leveled with Joanie's and she flashed a smile as they all clinked glasses. Again, she avoided looking at Wayne because she was embarrassed by Octavius's outspoken manner toward her.

"Let's venture outside, shall we?" Octavius led the way out the back door to the stunning deck, which was beautifully lit with small white lights hanging along the perimeter. "I don't think we got out here last time you dropped in. Make yourselves at home for the show." He meant the sunset, which was unfolding before their eyes.

Octavius bent to one knee and lit up a round gas fire table that was about five-feet in radius.

"How far back does your property go?" Wayne asked.

"Just to the small stone wall you see back there," Octavius said. "But the beautiful thing is, beyond that wall is the Coconino National Forest, which is comprised of a mere one-point-nine million acres of national preserve land. Not a bad view, right?"

The massive Red Rock Mountains were indeed right there. The setting sun made their vibrant colors pop.

Octavius grabbed a set of binoculars and handed them to Joanie. "Sometimes you can see climbers up there, but probably not this time of day. I shall return with hors d'oeuvres un momento." He dashed back into the house.

"Where's Suzanne?" Deetz said to Joanie.

She shrugged. "No idea. She hasn't texted me back. Can you believe this place?" Joanie looked around at the custom stonework which led from the huge grill and outdoor kitchen area to a small in-ground pool and hot tub. Bird feeders and water troughs of all shapes and sizes dotted the grounds.

"If this guy's an artist, his paintings must sell for thousands. What'd he do before he came here?" Wayne said.

"No idea." Joanie kept her voice down. "Suzanne said he's an entrepreneur. Ask him."

Octavius breezed out of the house somehow managing to carry

four trays. He came down and spread them along the top of the low stone wall of the fire table. "A bit of a charcuterie for my friends."

"Wow." Joanie's mouth began to water instantly.

"Each is labeled in chalk on the black slate and we have an assortment of cheeses, crackers, as well as breads and toast from a local business in which I am part owner," Octavius said. "There's also smoked salmon and some nice meats for you."

Joanie was impressed—and hungry. She helped herself to a slice of goat cheese on toast.

Octavius glanced at his Apple watch. "Where can she be? Pardon me friends while I run in and call our lady."

"Oh my gosh!" Joanie squealed and curled her feet up on her chair. She watched in horror as a small, hairy animal meandered toward them from the brush.

"Ha ha! Don't be frightened, Joanie, that's just a javelina," Octavius said. "One of many critters around here. They're our friends."

The animal slowly moved closer. "Are they dangerous?" Joanie was truly frightened.

Octavius laughed. "Not alone like that. He won't bother you. Let me ring Suzanne." He disappeared into the house.

As the critter approached Wayne he kicked at it and sneered, "Get out of here." It turned and slowly walked away.

"Be nice," Joanie said.

"I thought you were scared of it."

She peered through the binoculars as the sun set on the magnificent red and orange mountain range.

"This is stunning," Joanie said.

Octavius came back out. "Ah, Joanie, look up at the top—do you see the layers?"

"Yes," she said as she continued looking through the binoculars in wonder.

"That is known as the Hermit Formation. It's comprised of layers of sandstone, mudstone, and conglomerate—about two hundred and eighty million years old."

"Wow," she said, hoping Wayne didn't object aloud to the notion that the mountains were millions of years old, rather than their belief, based on a biblical timeline, that the earth was more like six- to fifteen-thousand years old.

"So, what did Suzanne say?" Deetz asked.

"Believe it or not, she's having car trouble," Octavius said. "But she's got a mobile mechanic on the way. We're hoping she can still make it—if not a little late."

"Too bad," Deetz said. "What's wrong with the car?"

Octavius shrugged. "No idea."

Joanie had lowered the binoculars and was looking at him now.

"I know a great deal about a great many things, but automobiles are not my forte," Octavius said.

"Hmm," Deetz said. "Well, would it not start? Did it break down someplace?"

Wayne was pressing the issue and it made Joanie feel uncomfortable, but she too would have appreciated more detail.

"We'll have to find out when she gets here, won't we?" Octavius sliced a large hunk of cheese, put it on a cracker with meat, and tossed it in his mouth. "Have you tried the prosciutto, Joanie?"

"Um, not yet."

"Out of this world," Octavius said with a mouthful. "Who needs more wine?"

"I need to use the restroom first," Deetz said.

"Perfect timing." Octavius waved his empty glass. "You can grab the wine while you're in there. Lavatory is first door on your left down the hallway. Wine's on the kitchen counter; bring the bottle. Thanks, Wayne."

"Sure thing." Wayne headed for the house and heard Octavius turn on the charm as he was going.

"Joanie, come. Take my hand. I must show you my new sculpture."

Her face flushed.

He had her hand.

She looked toward the house as they began to walk.

Wayne had stopped at the back door and was looking directly into her eyes.

4

Octavius relished these little mind games.

He led Joanie around the corner of the stone house, her soft hand in his. *Poor Deetz is probably having a conniption fit.*

"Oh, what's this?" Joanie pulled her hand away from his and pointed to the large black stone bowl full of water on the ground.

"That's for the deer . . . my dear." Octavius grinned at her with his most salacious smile. "And you see right here, on this post, is my night vision cam. It captures all kinds of absolutely insane activity out here in the middle of the night—coyotes, deer, racoons, even leopards."

"Oh, my. Really?"

Yes, really. And you should see what my other cameras capture.

"We'll have to hike while you're here," he said. "There are all kinds of trailheads nearby. The wildlife you see is uncanny. Snakes. Spiders. Lizards."

Joanie nodded shyly, obviously uncomfortable with him suggesting a hike. How he loved pushing her buttons.

"What's the farthest you've been on a hike away from the house?" she said.

He laughed to himself. She was nervous, just making small talk in attempt to sidetrack his advances.

"About nine miles out, nine miles back. That day I did the James

Trout Trail. Really a workout. But great for the old physique. Can you tell I work out, Joanie?"

She could only muster an awkward smile. She looked away as her cheeks exploded with color—a combination of alizarin crimson and cadmium red.

He grabbed her hand and veered off toward his camouflage-colored off-road four-wheeler. "Come on, we'll take the ATV."

She pulled her hand away and stopped. "I don't want to go without Wayne."

He laughed. "Okay. But it's just up on the ridge." He rubbed the top of his bald head and pointed toward the sculpture. "Right up there. We can walk, if you prefer."

She looked back toward the door where Deetz had gone in.

"Fish or cut bait, Joanie. Daylight's burning." Oh, how he enjoyed being so daringly in-your-face. It was a style that had evolved over the years and served him well. "Come on then, we'll walk." He started toward the ridge. "Wayne will see us and join up."

Joanie glanced back again toward the door, then onto the path leading toward the ridge where Octavius had pointed. "Okay."

"The work you're about to see is made completely of copper." He talked while they walked. "It took two years to create—and a lot of heavy lifting."

She said nothing but huffed along the dirt and stone trail about five feet behind him.

It was still light, but the sun was almost down and the temperature was dropping rapidly.

Octavius giggled to himself as he continued leading the way, anxious to see Joanie's reaction the second she laid her gorgeous eyes on the ten-foot sculpture of Venus, standing with her strong legs outstretched and her long arms reaching toward the sun.

He glanced back as he trudged up to the crest of the ridge. He could see Deetz had come out of the house and was sitting by the fire again. Octavius reached the statue slightly out of breath, turned around and waved for Deetz to join them, but Deetz did not acknowledge the gesture.

Joanie, too, reached the crest of the hill and waved for Deetz to come. But again, he acted as if he did not see them.

"Looks like he's comfortable where he is." Octavius turned to face the gleaming sculpture, which was catching the last of the Arizona sunset.

Joanie turned to look. Her eyebrows raised and her eyes opened wide. "Oh, wow. This is something."

Octavius could tell she was embarrassed, perhaps by some of the detail in Venus's nude physique.

"And you have a bench here and such pretty landscaping," she said.

She was changing the subject.

"You know who it is," he said.

"Venus."

"Correct." He took two giant steps toward Joanie, took her hand, and led her around the red gravel circle that surrounded the masterpiece. "When you sit on the bench . . . Come. Sit." He plopped down on the bench and she did so, hesitantly. She took her hand away. "I've designed it so that, at each stage of the sun rising in the east, when you sit here and look at the sun through the sculpture, the sun highlights various, shall we say, *aspects* or *qualities*, of the Roman goddess."

Joanie slowly nodded. "Interesting."

She was clearly embarrassed, and that thrilled Octavius.

"There's something about a Roman goddess, out here among these magical rocks, in this *hot* desert, reaching toward the sun. She is yearning for something. Longing. Aching."

Joanie stood abruptly. "I'm ready to go back."

Octavius roared with laughter. "What's wrong?" He stood. "You don't like my Venus?"

She started walking back down the trail and mumbled something he couldn't understand.

"Hold up." He hurried up behind her and took her elbow.

She pulled her arm away and continued focusing on the rocks and path beneath her feet.

"How long have you and Wayne been married?" Octavius said from behind.

"Thirty-four years."

"Gracious." *How could anyone remain with the same person that long?*

"What about you?" She continued walking ahead of him at a

good clip, obviously ready to be back with Deetz. "Have you ever been married?"

"Oh, holy horrors—never," he lied. "There are far too many Venuses out there for me to be tied down to one."

"What about Suzanne?" she said, as they drew within a few hundred feet of Deetz, who was sitting by the fire, scrolling through his phone. "She tells me you two are quite serious."

"Oh, we are, we are. But I think we both agree it's a romantic *friendship*, a really fun partnership. But neither of us want to be married. Egad. Never."

Joanie tilted her head and squinted back at him. "Really." It was a statement, not a question.

"Yes, *really*." Octavius wasn't about to let on that Suzanne was trapped square in the middle of his spiderweb (just like the others). One could even say she was 'addicted' to him.

"Have you heard anymore from Suzanne?" Deetz said as they approached.

Joanie looked at Octavius, who snatched the bottle of wine Deetz had brought out, looked at their still half-full glasses, and filled his own.

Octavius had been certain the last dosage of opioids he'd given Suzanne late that afternoon would put her in just the right mood for the dinner that evening, but something had gone amiss. Suzanne had gone into an odd tail spin and Octavius had been forced to quarantine her in the basement with the others. It was the very last thing he'd wanted to do, but he'd had no choice because the cursed Deetzes had arrived.

"Octavius?" Deetz said.

"No. Nothing more from our girl," he said, wondering if Suzanne was going to be coherent enough to make a brief appearance.

5

Deetz had to admit the Thai food Octavius served with such brimming pride was one of the best meals he'd ever eaten. The three of them sat at a sleek, light-colored wood and leather booth just off the huge room with the fireplace. The sky beyond the floor-to-ceiling windows was now black, but it was toasty warm in the low-lit house.

"I can't get enough of this stuff," Deetz whispered to Joanie. "Do you like it as much as I do?"

Joanie nodded and took another bite of the orange colored shrimp and noodles. "Delicious. I guess we need to find a Thai place back home."

"It won't be as good as this."

Octavius was in the wine cellar getting another bottle of vino. He'd pretty much polished the first one himself after pouring their initial glasses.

"This is weird without Suzanne," Joanie whispered.

"Tell me about it. I can't believe he took your hand out there."

"I know." She shook her head and her eyes searched the room with a sour look. "Something doesn't feel right."

"What do you mean?"

"Suzanne hasn't even called or texted me."

"She's probably busy with the mechanic."

"I don't know. She could easily shoot me a text."

Deetz heard footsteps on the stairs to the cellar and nodded to Joanie that Octavius was coming back.

"That was Suzanne." Octavius announced as he came into the room holding his phone up in one hand and a bottle of red wine in the other. "The mechanic got stuck in traffic, then got lost. She needed a new alternator." He opened the bottle at the bar. "The red wine will provide us with a nice finish—and perhaps a cigar by the fire?" He poured three new glasses and set them on the table.

"So, is her car fixed? Is she coming?" Joanie said.

"Oh, forgive me. No. I'm sorry. The mechanic had to drive to get the alternator. Traffic in town was a nightmare. Then he had to drive back to her place, then put it on. He's almost finished, but she's going to take a raincheck on tonight. She's just spent and she thinks it's too late to come. I'm sorry. Looks like you're stuck with just me for tonight."

Joanie and Deetz glanced at each other, then both said it was fine and remarked again about the flavor of the food. It was an awkward few moments.

"So, have you always been an artist?" Deetz said.

Octavius patted his mouth with the thick, white cloth napkin and grinned; his smile was attractive and resembled that of a female, because of his thin lips. "I've always loved it, ever since I was a boy. My mom was an artist, of sorts; she did amazing block prints. The detail was uncanny. I've got some of them around here . . . Anyway, so I've worked at it all my life, but only began doing it full-time when I moved here."

"And what did you do in—St. Augustine, wasn't it?" Joanie asked.

Octavius rubbed his shiny head with his large right hand. "Good memory, sweet Joanie. I was actually in the boat business."

He stopped with that and Deetz was surprised he offered no more detail.

"Did you *sell* boats?" Deetz pursued it, because what else were they going to talk about?

Octavius carefully fingered each corner of his mouth with the napkin, set it on the table as if declaring the meal was over, and smiled that charming smile. "I guess that's the detective in you, coming out." He laughed. "Yes, we sold luxury yachts."

Again, there was silence. Octavius obviously didn't want to share more about his boat dealings.

"So, you mentioned you're part-owner of a what, a bread company?" Joanie said.

Octavius nodded, but looked put off. "Indeed. It's just a small plant where we make our own artisan breads—sourdough, ciabatta, brioche. You had some of our country loaf as your appetizer. Now . . . " He stood, leaned over, and squeezed out of the richly upholstered booth. "Shall we retreat to the fire table for a cigar? Or, is it going to be too cold out there for you?"

Deetz checked his watch. The night was still fairly young and he really didn't want to sit around the tiny house all evening; besides, Octavius was one intriguing character. He looked at Joanie. "You up for staying a bit?"

Joanie raised her eyebrows and shrugged. Deetz could tell she didn't want to stay.

"Come on, lovely lady." Octavius grasped her arm. "I'll put on the heater for you out there. And if you need another wrap, I've got several of Suzanne's coats in the closet. Would you like one?"

"Oh no. I'll be fine. Thanks."

Again, Deetz could tell Joanie was ready to go home.

"Okay then, whatever you say." Octavius rubbed his hands together. "Let me grab some cigars from the humidor. Joanie, will you be joining us? They're Cuban."

She laughed and said no.

Octavius disappeared down the hallway.

"I can't believe you said you wanted to stay." Joanie scowled at Wayne.

"When do I ever get to try a Cuban cigar? Besides, this guy is pure entertainment."

"Let's not stay long." She stood and collected several plates. "We should clear the dishes."

Deetz helped her and they got everything off the table in no time. While Joanie rinsed the plates and loaded them into the dishwasher, Wayne wandered around the large living room, examining the many paintings, photographs, and evil looking tribal masks hanging on the walls.

Deetz stopped and stared at one of the paintings because it was so striking. It was a brown, antique-looking door with a small, square window which featured a purple reflection of a woman's face, barely noticeable. Bright colors around the dark door—yellows, oranges, whites, and grays—made the door pop in vivid contrast. It was somewhat haunting. Octavius had signed his name in the lower right corner with a huge, looping 'O' and 'H' to start his first and last name. Deetz leaned close to examine the keyhole of the door and etched inside was a name: Delia.

"Hey." Joanie had turned off the water and was whispering loudly to Wayne across the room. "Are you feeling anything from that wine?"

"What do you mean?" Deetz said.

"I only drank a few sips and I feel kind of cloudy."

Deetz laughed. "He probably slipped something in yours."

Her shoulders slumped exaggeratedly and she glared at him. "I'm not drinking any more, I'll tell you that."

A long shadow crossed the floor. "You're not drinking anymore, Joanie?" It was Octavius, holding the cigars. "Why not? That Pinot is an impeccable choice—from Cote de Nuits."

Joanie looked shell-shocked and Deetz could only snicker to himself. *Let's see how she gets out of this.*

"Oh, it's fine, I'm sure. No, I was just telling Wayne I was feeling a little . . . light-headed. Probably haven't drank enough water—with all the hiking we've been doing." She glanced at Wayne. He smiled and nodded slightly. *Nicely played.*

"Grab a glass in the cupboard above the toaster oven," Octavius said. "There's a tap with purified water built into the front of the fridge. You must keep hydrated. My yoga instructor is big, big, big on that."

"So, I noticed this painting of the door." Deetz pointed to the canvas on the wall and walked toward it.

"You like that one?" Octavius said.

"It's striking," Deetz said. "I noticed the name Delia in the keyhole. What's the significance of that?"

Octavius bristled and glared at Deetz for a split-second before snapping out of it and turning on the charm again. "Ah, you really are the investigator aren't you, Detective Deetz?" He laughed heartily. "Actually that painting was a commissioned piece for a couple in Denmark; I suppose her name was Delia—I don't recall." He threw up his hands and raised his dark eyebrows. "Anyway, they didn't like it! But, I happened to love it, so here it is."

"Did you do another one for them?" Joanie asked from the kitchen.

"I did not, even though they wanted me to," Octavius said. "And I kept the first installment."

"The metal sculpture over there," Deetz pointed to the piece of art high on the wall in the living room. "StoneSpell. You mentioned that before. Is that the name of the house or property here?"

Octavius found his wine glass and leaned into the kitchen. "Joanie, please stop. I'll take care of all that clean up later. I want you to hear this."

"It's done. I'm coming." She dried her hands and joined them in the living room.

"This home was built by an award-winning architect. Internationally-known. Wolfgang Brandt. You probably haven't heard of him. His homes are often featured in *Architectural Digest* and all the big publications."

Of course, poor, uncultured Wayne and Joanie Deetz wouldn't have heard of him. Way above our pay- and culture-scale.

"Anyway, he built this place for himself in 2012. But he was so busy working and traveling the world that he rarely came here."

Joanie began to say something, but Octavius cut her off.

"But when he did get here he said he experienced the most euphoric, mystic, rejuvenating *powers* he'd ever known. And he attributed it to the red rocks, the vortices. In fact, he said he picked this very plot of land for the house because he'd researched the geography and the native American history, and determined it was an area of concentrated supernatural power and spiritual energy where people could access altered states of consciousness. He told me this himself when I bought the place. That's why he'd named it StoneSpell."

It sounded like a bunch of horse manure to Deetz. "So, why did he sell the place if it was so . . . magical?" he said.

Octavius squinted at Deetz with a look of spitefulness. "Well, like I said, he was a busy man. He has homes all over the world. But there's no arguing, this is sacred land. It holds ancient wisdom.

Some days it literally crackles with energy." His gaze fell to Joanie and he stared at her—way too long.

She blushed and looked away.

It angered Deetz.

"Do you really believe the rocks this place is built on are any different than the soil my house sits on in Portland?" Deetz said, taking a seat on the small brick wall next to the fireplace.

"Wayne." Joanie shot him a mean look as if to stop him from being negative.

"Ha. Are you kidding me, Wayne? The vortices in Sedona have proven to be intersections of natural electromagnetic earth energy." Octavius plunked down in a light-colored leather chair near Deetz. "They are swirling sources of power conducive to healing and spiritual enlightenment. Brandt, the architect, told me himself that StoneSpell sits on land that exudes *masculine* energy, in fact."

Deetz put a hand over his mouth, trying to hide his disdain. Joanie blinked slowly and shook her head ever so slightly, signaling for him to keep his mouth shut.

"Masculine energy, huh?" Deetz said.

Joanie clenched her teeth and gave him an angry look.

"That's right. I work with a spiritual mentor, kind of like a personal trainer or coach, but we work on deep spiritual connections. Joanie, won't you sit?" Octavius patted the leather ottoman next to him.

"I think I'll sit by the fire, it's so toasty." She sat on the brick ledge, opposite Wayne and the fireplace.

"It's all about radical self-care. We do things that nourish the conscious mind and honor the miraculous body." Octavius spoke in an almost seductive tone—watching closely for Joanie's reaction.

Deetz was speechless. He knew he better not say anything, because whatever he would say would come out negative.

"I work with this amazing woman on an individual basis. We have our sessions right out amid the red rocks at some of Sedona's most active vortices—Bell Rock, Airport Mesa, Boynton Canyon, etcetera. Sometimes we work right out back here."

Octavius looked at each of them, back and forth. "You don't believe in the type of spiritual formation I'm talking about, do you?" He smirked and sensually smelled one of the cigars.

"Suzanne told me you're Christians. She used to attend a church in town. I grew up in the church. Frankly, though, I never saw any fruit from it. Not like what I get when I meet with Miracle—that's the woman's name, my spiritual coach. She uses things like movement, relaxation techniques, connections with others, and the healing arts to bring about—how can I describe it? It's bliss, really. I know it will sound cocky, but I am the most joyful and contented person I know!"

What a fruit loop.

"Has Suzanne shown any interest in joining you?" Joanie said.

Deetz knew Joanie feared Octavius was brainwashing Suzanne with his mysticism.

Octavius frowned and stuck his nose in the air as if smelling a rotten banana. "What I have with Miracle and our sessions is for me. It's self-care. I wouldn't want to share that space with Suzanne —or anyone. Now, having said that, I have encouraged her to take a session or two with Miracle on her own, and I think she's going to do that soon. I hope she will."

Deetz was contemplating what he could say to further discuss the topic of faith and Christianity when Octavius suddenly stood. "I'm afraid it's too cold out there tonight to enjoy these fine sticks. Wayne, would you care to take yours with you?"

Wayne took the hint that it was time to leave and stood as well. "No, thank you very much. Save it for next time."

Joanie got up, too. "Thank you so much for dinner, Octavius. It was incredible."

"It really was," Deetz said, going to get their coats from the back of a chair across the room.

"Oops," Octavius looked startled, then reached into his pocket and answered his phone. "My dear, how are you?" He looked at Wayne and Joanie and whispered, "It's Suzanne!" Then he wandered into the kitchen, speaking to her as Joanie and Wayne got on their coats.

"We had a marvelous dinner together. Joanie went up to see Venus with me." With that, Octavius swirled around and winked at Joanie, then spoke into the phone again. "Is the car all fixed? Good, good. What's that? I will tell them you'll talk to them tomorrow.

Oh and darling, we've got scads of leftovers, so please plan to enjoy some tomorrow."

Deetz and Joanie started toward the door.

Octavius held up a finger and whispered to them, "Just one moment. I'll walk out with you."

Deetz leaned close to Joanie's ear and said, "I don't think he's talking to anyone."

6

Joanie drank almost a whole bottle of water when she and Wayne got back to the tiny house at 8:40 p.m., but she still couldn't shake the fog she was in and could only trust it would be gone by morning. She was quite sure it was just a combination of the high altitude, dehydration, and perhaps the tiny bit of wine she'd had at dinner.

She threw her robe on over her pajamas, grabbed Wayne's laptop, and curled up on the couch in the little living room to do some snooping.

Deetz came out of the bedroom wearing sweats and a hoodie, carrying his Kindle. He went into the kitchen and flipped on the light. "Heard from her yet?"

"Nope." Joanie had tried to call Suzanne on the way home from Octavius's house, thinking she would reach her, because Octavius had just spoken to her—or so he said. But Wayne insisted Octavius had been faking the call.

"Why would he pretend to be talking to her?" Joanie said.

"Who knows? Maybe for the same reason he has hidden cameras in the house."

"What? What are you saying?"

"I saw what I'm almost positive was a hidden camera—in the kitchen, hidden in an outlet."

"Are you for real?"

Deetz nodded, wide-eyed. "If I'm not wrong, there was another one above the front door."

"He showed me a camera out back," Joanie said. "He said it captured the deer and other animals drinking out of the water bowl."

"Who knows? Let's not plan on seeing this guy again, can we do that?"

"I just can't understand why Suzanne's not responding to my calls or texts?" Joanie said. "It's plain weird. She was so excited about us coming out here. She had all kinds of plans for us."

"And we've seen her once," Deetz said.

"I told you she wasn't herself. What could be going on, Wayne? Seriously."

"I can't believe she fell for this guy." Deetz stepped in from the kitchen with his own plastic water bottle.

"I know why. She's always loved the arts. She's always loved nice things, quality things—"

"Expensive things."

"Right. And here comes this handsome, single guy who's all of those."

"Yeah, but the tradeoff. I mean, he's so full of himself," Deetz said. "And all that about the earth energy and swirling powers and his new age guru, *Miracle*." He pronounced her name as if introducing a performer. "I mean, Suzanne's a Christian, right? How can she be falling for this stuff?"

"Wayne, stop. Listen to yourself. You sound so self-righteous."

"I'm just saying, the guy is the complete opposite of a Christian; Suzanne's got to see that."

"Okay, we don't know all the details. Sometimes you can be so judgmental."

Silence.

"I'm searching him." Joanie typed 'Octavius Hunt' into the online search engine.

"This'll be interesting." Deetz plopped down in the recliner, tilted it back, and turned on his Kindle.

Joanie drained her water bottle, crunched it, and set it on the end table.

"He wasn't afraid to come onto you right in front of me," Deetz said.

"It made the hair on the back of my neck stand straight up. Gross."

"Must be all the 'masculine energy' bubbling up from under the house." Deetz laughed at his own joke as he settled into his chair to read.

Joanie's search led her to the official Octavius Hunt website. It featured a large, professional portrait photograph of him, along with a comprehensive gallery showing dozens of his paintings and sculptures, ranging from $750 to $30,000. There was no bio, no blog, no way to connect with him. She told Deetz about the site and kept searching.

The only image that came up for Octavius Hunt was the same one from his website, in which he's sitting on a stool in his studio wearing a dark wool beret and scarf, a turtleneck shirt and plaid vest, jeans, and the same leather shoes he was wearing when they saw him earlier that evening. He cradled a smoking pipe in his large hands.

Joanie could find no videos of Octavius and the few articles she did find were about his recent artwork and the classes he taught at the studio in Jessup. "This is downright weird. He's not on Twitter or Facebook. His Instagram account's only been around eight months and it's the same content as his website. It's like he didn't even exist before he came to Sedona."

"Put his name and St. Augustine," Deetz said.

"I did!"

"Try his name and luxury boats, yachts, and—"

"I've tried everything." The wheels in Joanie's mind were spinning. "There's nothing showing him in St. Augustine. There's nothing showing Octavius Hunt existed prior to two years ago."

"That is odd." Deetz readjusted in the recliner.

"I found the architect, Wolfgang Brandt, and that story pans out —about the house," Joanie said. "There was an article about it in some architectural magazine."

"Still nothing from Suzanne?" Deetz said.

Joanie glanced at her phone. "Not a peep."

"Hmm. You want me to look?"

She got up and took him the laptop. "You're not going to find anything."

Deetz started tapping away at the keyboard, searching the internet.

Joanie checked her phone again. "It's still early. Maybe we should run over there."

"Where?" Deetz looked up at her with his mouth hanging open and a sour look on his face.

"Suzanne's place."

Deetz groaned and rolled his eyes. "Honey, we're in for the night. That bed is calling me."

"Something's not right, Wayne. I know it. I know Suzanne. This is not like her to not communicate."

Deetz stared at the laptop screen and continued clicking away. "Just hold on."

"There's nothing there, Wayne. Come on. Let's run over there. It'll take fifteen minutes."

Deetz swayed back and forth wearily, and pretended to collapse, closing the laptop as he slumped over.

"I'm going, whether you come or not." Joanie headed for the bedroom to start getting dressed, knowing there was no way Wayne would let her go without him.

7

With the bottle of red wine and a half-full glass on the desk in front of him, Octavius puffed away at his pipe and carefully examined each of the high-def color monitors glowing in front of him in the dark basement control center, which he liked to think of as Ground Zero.

There were twelve monitors in all, neatly mounted on the wall, each connected to cameras and highly sensitive condenser microphones hidden throughout the house and grounds of StoneSpell. Off to the right were two more monitors that would show any activity inside Suzanne's apartment. Of course, they were still now, because she was not there.

Octavius sipped from the big glass and began viewing footage from the Deetz's arrival at StoneSpell earlier that evening. He watched as they joined hands and approached the house with Deetz mumbling about how expensive Octavius's Benz must be. Then he heard Joanie wondering aloud about where Suzanne's car was.

Octavius smirked and fired up his pipe again. This was pure entertainment for him; it was like his ultimate sweet spot. He fast-forwarded as the guests admired the interior of the house and made their way to the back patio area. When he found the segment where he handed Joanie the binoculars and went into the house to get the hors d'oeuvres, he let the video and audio play as Deetz questioned where Suzanne was. Then he estimated how much Octavius's paintings must sell for and wondered aloud what Octavius did before he moved to Sedona.

The dangerous curiosity of a cop.

Pipe in mouth, Octavius squinted through the smoke and clicked and scrolled until he came to the footage inside the house, when Deetz entered to use the bathroom and retrieve the bottle of wine. On the screen, Deetz slid the glass door shut and scanned the room. He walked to the kitchen, picked up the bottle of wine, examined it, and set it down. Then he headed down the hallway toward the bathroom.

Octavius changed cameras and watched as Deetz peered into the first door on his left, the bathroom, but then practically tip-toed further down the hall, looking into Octavius's master bedroom, then into the adjacent room, the home studio. Deetz entered that room. Octavius quickly switched to the home studio camera. Deetz walked the perimeter of the room, looking closely at several of the works on the walls, and even picked up a framed photograph of Octavius; it was the one of him and Jessup Mayor Marsden Maddox and his wife, Candace.

Octavius couldn't really blame Deetz for snooping; he would do the same thing. He fast-forwarded the footage of Deetz walking back down the hall, entering the restroom, coming out, and walking into the kitchen for the bottle of wine.

"Ohhhh, looky here," Octavius said aloud and inched closer to one of the screens after seeing Deetz do a double-take and stare right into the lens of the hidden camera. "Oh my goodness, aren't we observant?" He watched breathlessly as Deetz walked directly toward the camera, which was hidden behind a stone wall outlet, its lens half the size of a dime. Deetz looked around the house to make sure no one was watching, then bent down and leaned his big head and smudged glasses ten inches from the camera. Octavius watched dumbfounded. Then Deetz gave a small wave and said, "Lovely place you have here," and he grabbed the bottle of wine and went outside.

Octavius backed away from the screen, slowly shook his head, and uncomfortably debated whether he could've underestimated Deetz. After all, the old codger had somehow found Delia's name etched in the painting of the door. *No one's ever noticed that!* He took another gulp of wine, set the pipe in the ashtray, and found the clip of the next segment of the evening when Deetz and Joanie were alone. It was when they were all eating dinner and Octavius used the excuse of going to the wine cellar in order to check on Suzanne's status.

He played the footage. Deetz and Joanie raved about Octavius's cooking, then Joanie commented on how weird it was Suzanne was not with them. When Deetz expressed his disbelief that Octavius had held Joanie's hand, Octavius laughed so hard he had an uncontrollable coughing spell and had to pause the playback.

Octavius pushed his chair back, went to a nearby table, grabbed a tissue, and blew his nose. For the first time, he was feeling slightly uneasy about the Deetzes. He went back to the monitors and clicked play while still standing. Joanie said to Deetz, something didn't feel right. *A woman's intuition—never good.* Octavius sat down and watched as Joanie expressed her concern about Suzanne not responding to her attempts to reach her.

Octavius took his pipe and lighter, and leaned back in the luxurious black leather office chair. He lit the bowl, got the pipe smoking, and tossed the lighter on the desk.

This could be trouble. Probably not, but possibly.

He needed to get Suzanne clearheaded—enough to spend a bit of time with Joanie to get her off his case.

But is that possible? In her state, she's liable to blow it.

The first time the women had seen each other Suzanne could barely keep her eyes open. Octavius had kept Joanie and Wayne as occupied as possible in hopes they wouldn't notice Suzanne's abnormal demeanor.

If I don't get Suzanne in shape, the Deetzes will be a problem.

A dark thought crossed his mind like a shadow—he may need to make the Deetzes disappear on their little jaunt to Sedona.

You're getting way ahead of yourself.

Octavius continued the video and watched proudly as he returned to dinner with the bottle of red and explained the lie that Suzanne was having car trouble.

Not only am I an amazing actor, I look really good in that denim shirt. Note to self—order another one in black.

Octavius watched closely as the playback showed him leaving

the room for the cigars. Joanie whispered her disbelief that Wayne had wanted to stay longer. They cleared the dishes. Octavius fast-forwarded until he noticed Joanie speaking. He hit play just in time to hear her ask Deetz if he was feeling anything from the wine.

Octavius snickered, then laughed even more when Joanie mentioned feeling 'cloudy.' *You haven't seen anything yet, lovely Joanie.*

On the playback, Deetz then jested that perhaps Octavius had put something in her drink.

Octavius hit 'stop.'

The picture froze.

He leaned in and examined balding Deetz, with his dirty glasses and old-fashioned baggy jeans and Walmart fake leather shoes.

That portion of the playback should have relieved Octavius, because Deetz obviously didn't have a clue that he really had slipped some powdered oxycontin into Joanie's wine. But instead, it infuriated him. He downed the rest of the wine in his glass, poured more, and clacked the bottle down on the glass desk.

All of a sudden, Wayne Deetz was really bothering Octavius.

Who does he think he is, coming in my home, demeaning me, slandering me?

Octavius scrolled and clicked until he came to the final portion of the video, when his guests were leaving and he was faking the phone call with Suzanne. He leaned in and watched closely the expressions on Wayne's and Joanie's faces as he rambled on with the phone to his ear, pretending to update Suzanne on the evening.

Joanie seemed to be going right along with it as they headed for the door. But Deetz was a different story. He was eye-balling Octavius the entire time. He'd whispered something to Joanie that Octavius hadn't been able to hear when it happened. Now, Octavius turned up the volume and leaned within a foot of the monitor, watching as Deetz whispered to Joanie: "I don't think he's talking to anyone."

Octavius lurched and cursed at the top of his lungs. He stood abruptly and drained the rest of the wine in his glass. He lifted the bottle to his lips, threw his head back, finished the bottle, and heaved it at the side wall with an enormous explosion of glass. He cursed again and smacked the main power button and watched as all the monitors flicked to black.

Silence.

There was no way he was about to allow a washed-up cop from Portland to ruin his luxurious, opulent way of life.

If he finds out about Suzanne, he finds out about the others . . . right on the opposite side of that wine-stained wall.

"That's not going to happen," Octavius said as he quickly exited Ground Zero, shut the bronze-colored metal door behind him, headed down the hallway, and turned to face the sleek wood staircase leading back upstairs.

He stood for a moment, formulating a plan.

Go in, get Suzanne, get her back to her place, do whatever you have to do to get her ready to spend a small amount of time with Joanie and Deetz tomorrow—even just fifteen minutes. Have her tell them a relative died or something and that she's got to leave town. Then, bring her back here and administer more fentanyl. End of the Deetz saga.

And if that didn't work, it would be hike time with the Deetzes at Black Summit Trail, where many had fallen to their deaths—both accidentally, and by design; not by his hand, but there was a first time for everything.

With that, Octavius bent down, gripped the bottom step of the staircase with both hands, and lifted with a grunt. Half of the staircase, about nine feet worth, arose easily with a slight hiss thanks to the hydraulic lift supports on each side. When the stairs locked in place above his head, Octavius ducked underneath and headed for another bronze metal door—this one, hidden from the view of all visitors.

He slid the bottom bolt lock open with a loud click, then the one in the middle of the door, then the one at the top.

He'd hated to put Suzanne in there for the first time, but it had been his only option. He couldn't let the Deetzes see her during her oxy-induced high. He knew he was going to have a lot of explaining to do to her later.

He took a deep breath, pulled the heavy door open, stepped in and shined the light from his phone. Usually when he came for one of them, they were scared by the noise, startled by the brightness, and fearful of his intimidating presence.

On the left, Janine turned beneath her bed covers and peeked out with blinking red eyes, her brown hair a mess. She mumbled some sort of plea and her head dropped back on the pillow.

Octavius shined his light to the right, Delia's bed. She was out to the world.

Neither of them had the strength or clarity to do anything, to put up a fight, to try to get away.

He entered further into the darkness, shining his light toward the bed at the far end of the chamber. "Suzanne," he shouted above a whisper. "Wake up. Wake up, *now*."

8

"Man, it gets cold here at night; I had no idea," Deetz said as he drove the rental SUV toward Suzanne's place at about 9:20 p.m. He'd kept on his sweats and hoodie, and had thrown on some running shoes in place of his slippers. "I need a hat. My bald head is freezing."

"I told you the forecast before we left," Joanie said. "Do you remember me telling you it gets down to freezing here at night?" Joanie had changed from her pajamas into black leggings, sneakers, a sweater, and jacket, and was keeping a close watch on the GPS on the dash. "Do you remember, or are you going senile?"

They both laughed.

"How much farther?" Deetz said.

"I'm not going to answer that, Wayne. The GPS is right in front of you."

"The numbers on it are so small—"

"Do you hear yourself?"

They laughed again.

"You sound like a decrepit old man. Turn right in one mile and we're there. My gosh. This is like driving with a hundred-year-old."

It was getting late and they were both giddy.

Deetz was tired and looking forward to sleeping in the bed at the tiny house again. It had a luxurious mattress and a huge, thick white down comforter. He'd slept better in Sedona than he had in months at home.

Probably because you're not working.

"We should get a down comforter just like the one at the tiny house," he said.

"You say that now, but we'll get home, I'll find one and you'll say it's too expensive."

"Ha! You're probably right."

If his sleep pattern in Sedona was any indicator of what retired life would be like, he may be ready for it sooner rather than later. He trusted God would show him clearly on this trip.

It was a cold, clear night. There wasn't nearly the traffic in Red Rock City as there had been in Sedona. The streets were clean and well-maintained, with a fifteen-foot median filled with red gravel, cactus, and an assortment of desert plants, some of which were decorated with white lights for the holidays.

"Okay, right here on Dearborn, then an immediate right into her complex," Joanie said, sitting up toward the front of her seat.

Deetz made the right, spotted the lighted sign for Adobe Village Apartments, and pulled in. "What number?"

"Five-fifty-two."

Deetz examined the sign showing numbers and arrows.

"To the right." Joanie beat him to it.

He veered right and drove slowly through the parking lot, which was quite full of cars. It was a weeknight. People were in for the night.

"I think that's her car." Joanie pointed to a small white Kia.

He pulled into a space several spots away from it, parked, and turned off the car.

"Let's take a peek at the car." Deetz began to get out and so did Joanie. They walked over to the car and Deetz felt the hood. "Cold."

Joanie cupped her hands and peered in through the passenger window. Deetz looked in on the other side. There was nothing unusual. They looked at each other across the top of the car.

"May as well go up and knock," Deetz said. "If it's awkward I can just stay outside."

Joanie agreed with a nod and they walked toward the five-hundred building, one of five similar structures situated in the shape of a horseshoe. Each two-story building was constructed of red stucco and included about twenty units. They were blockish looking buildings. It appeared each unit had its own patio or balcony. A big tree between the two buildings they headed for was decorated in blinking, colored lights.

"What was the number?" Deetz said.

"This way." Joanie went ahead of him.

They walked down a breezeway past other doors marked in the five-hundreds.

"Five-fifty-two," Joanie said as they arrived at Suzanne's door.

Deetz pressed the doorbell and they looked at each other as they heard it chime.

He heard no movement inside.

Joanie took several steps to a window just to the left of the door. Its plastic blinds were closed and it appeared there was a small lamp on just beyond it.

Deetz quietly and gently tried the doorknob, but it was locked.

He rang the bell again.

After a few seconds he knocked.

Nothing.

"Why don't you try to call her again," he said.

Without a word, Joanie got her phone out and dialed Suzanne.

Deetz pressed an ear against the door, thinking he might hear the phone ring, but he heard nothing.

They waited in silence.

"No answer." Joanie put her phone away. "Maybe we can go around to her patio. Maybe we can see in."

Deetz frowned.

"Come on, honey," Joanie said. "We're here. We may as well be thorough."

The complex was quiet. Deetz saw no harm in trying.

"Okay." He led the way back where they'd come from but turned down a short breezeway that led to an open space where the other sides of the units could be accessed.

They held hands and walked back toward Suzanne's unit, passing one apartment that was dark, another with a colorfully lit Christmas tree, and another with lights on inside, but drapes drawn.

Joanie had counted them and pointed to the patio she'd determined was Suzanne's. They headed toward it, slowly, looking around to make sure no one saw them snooping.

They walked across the stone patio, past a small table and two chairs, to the sliding glass doors. Suzanne's drapes were open about four feet. They stood next to each other, cupped their hands, and peered inside. It looked like the one lone lamp by the window at the door may be the only light on inside.

The place was clean and organized. There was a dark couch with a chair next to it, a square coffee table, bookshelves, and a small TV. Books and magazines were stacked neatly in a wood bin next to the chair. There was a small dining room table beyond the living room, and the kitchen was beyond that, near the door they had tried. Not a single Christmas decoration, which seemed weird.

"I don't get it," Joanie whispered.

"Uh-uh. Come on, we better go."

"Wait." Joanie knocked on the glass door. "I just want to make sure."

Deetz looked around for nosey neighbors but saw none.

There was no movement inside.

"She can't be in there," Joanie said, with her face right up to the glass.

"No." Deetz was trying to be patient, letting Joanie exhaust every option. "Come on, babe. We should go."

They walked back around the patios, through the breezeway, and out to the parking lot.

Deetz was thinking, the only way Suzanne could be in there was if she had ear plugs in, was knocked out on sleep meds, or worse—but he wasn't about to say that to Joanie.

"Where could she be?" Joanie whispered.

"Maybe she's shacking up with the artist extraordinaire," Deetz said as he unlocked the car and opened Joanie's door for her. She got in and he walked to the driver's side and got in.

"It's not funny, Wayne. I'm seriously getting worried."

Deetz started the car and turned up the heat.

"I know. I don't get it, either. But we're going to get to the bottom of it. Don't worry, honey."

"I am worried."

"Can you get this thing to point us back home?" Deetz waved at the GPS.

"You don't remember?" She leaned closer and pressed a button. "All you have to do is hit the 'home' button—it's right here." She pointed at it. "I've got the tiny house programmed as home. Wayne, are you listening?"

"Hold up, hold up. Look!" Deetz sat as still as he could as he watched Octavius's shiny silver Mercedes wheel into a parking space fifty feet from them and jerk to a stop, lights going out. "It's him. Be still." Deetz turned the car off, reached over and took Joanie's hand without taking his eyes off the Mercedes. "Don't bend down or anything. Just be still. He can't spot us from here."

There were enough cars between them to shield them, Deetz thought.

The windows of the Mercedes were black, so they couldn't see inside.

They both sat speechless, watching as Octavius unfolded out of the car, slammed his door, and hurried around to the passenger side.

9

Joanie could barely breathe as she sat frozen in the rental car under the clear night sky, watching Octavius open the passenger door of the silver Mercedes, scan the parking lot, then lean inside. As he brought Suzanne to her feet outside the car and shut the door, Joanie let out a whimper.

"Shhh!" Wayne cupped a cold hand over her mouth as Joanie watched Suzanne wobble and struggle to take her first steps. Suzanne looked like a child whose grandmother had dressed her for school, with a long sweater that draped to the back of her knees, jeans, Crocs, and a thick knit hat pulled way down over her forehead and ears. But there was no mistaking it was her.

Octavius had one arm around her waist and his other hand clenched her arm, as if he was doing eighty percent of the work holding her up. They walked together, carefully, as if he was helping a 95-year-old invalid shuffle off to her porch rocker.

Wayne gently withdrew his hand from Joanie's mouth. "Be real quiet," he whispered.

Octavius dropped something. They stopped. He looked down. It was his keys. He balanced Suzanne, as if steadying a leaning tower of blocks. When he bent down for the keys, she swayed. He swooped the keys up and grabbed her or she would have collapsed to the pavement.

Joanie instinctively let out a yelp.

"No!" Wayne whispered, cupping her mouth again.

But this time, Octavius heard it. He looked in their direction and froze. Then he searched the parking lot as if his head was on a swivel.

"Stay still," Deetz whispered. "Don't move."

Joanie's heart bashed in her ribcage.

Is Suzanne drunk?

Where are they coming from?

Octavius's head stopped turning and he focused like a laser on Joanie and Wayne.

"Don't move," Deetz said, barely opening his mouth.

Joanie could see Octavius's breath huffing in the cold night air. He slowly raised his head, almost as if acknowledging them, then turned and resumed helping Suzanne.

Joanie could hear them speak briefly as they continued their slow walk toward the breezeway and Suzanne's apartment.

When they disappeared into the shadows, Joanie turned to Wayne. "We've got to go in there."

"Wait, honey. Just let me think." Wayne stared straight ahead.

"Did he see us?" Joanie said.

"Not sure. He may have."

"You think she's drunk?"

"Or drugged."

"We've got to help her, Wayne. Come on." Joanie opened her door.

"Wait." Deetz grabbed her arm.

Joanie stared at him with the door still open.

"We can approach this two ways," Wayne said. "Close your door."

Hesitantly, she squeezed it shut. "Talk fast."

"I can go to her door, but I don't have my gun or badge—and you're not coming."

Joanie protested, but Wayne cut her off.

"There's no sense in both of us going. If he's dangerous, we're not putting you in harm's way. The other thing we can do is let it go for tonight—"

"What are you saying?"

"He may not have seen us. She looked like she's going to be okay. And we'll see her tomorrow. You get alone with her and find out what's going on then."

"No way, we're not waiting. You can go alone if you want, but we have to make sure she's okay. I don't care what he thinks."

Deetz opened his door, but hesitated.

He didn't have his gun because they'd flown to Phoenix and he didn't want to put it in his luggage; he left the badge thinking he certainly wouldn't need it.

"Just tell Octavius we were concerned about her and came over," Joanie said. "Because she wasn't answering my calls."

"Okay." Deetz turned and looked intently into her eyes. "I want you to come over and get in the driver's seat." He started the car. "If I don't come out or call or text you within ten minutes I want you to call 911, give Suzanne's address, tell them there's a hostage situation; that'll get them here quick. Okay? Come around."

He started to get out, but Joanie grabbed his arm. "Pray, Wayne."

Deetz held her hand and quickly prayed for Suzanne's wellbeing, and for protection for he and Joanie.

They squeezed hands and Joanie got out and hurried around to the driver's side of the SUV. She got in and moved the seat up. Deetz looked at his phone. "Ten minutes from now will be 10:15 exactly. What are you going to do?"

She looked up at him, her heart racing. "Call nine-one-one, give the address, tell them there's a hostage situation."

"Right. And if he should come out here without me, you take off. Call nine-one-one," Deetz said. "Go to the police, not back to our place."

She nodded. "Be careful."

He closed her door, turned, and began walking fast toward the building.

Joanie watched him go and questioned herself for insisting he do so. He was almost sixty years old, recovering from a concussion, on vacation—what was she thinking?

If anything happens to him, it's your fault.

Suddenly, she wanted to stop him.
She flashed the lights.
But he didn't notice. He kept walking.
She was about to beep the horn when he disappeared into the breezeway.

10

Octavius was furious. This was not like him to be dashing around in the middle of the night frantically covering his tracks. It was beneath him.

Blast it!

He was almost certain it was Deetz and Joanie he'd seen watching him in the parking lot—which meant they'd likely be coming to check on Suzanne any minute. They were proving to be much more of a thorn in his side than he'd anticipated.

"We're almost there. Just a little farther." He hurried Suzanne along as fast as possible, but she was slogging along as if she were drunk.

"My gosh . . . what's the hurry?" she slurred. "Take it easy, will you?"

Octavius realized he needed to be very calculated about what he said to Suzanne—and how he played this. As far as she knew, she and Octavius were fine. He continued to wine and dine her and feed her a steady dose of opioids, which her life had come to depend upon, and she pretty much did anything he wanted, thanks to the drugs' euphoric effects.

Suzanne did not hold a job, at Octavius's insistence. He paid for everything in her life—rent, clothes, food, car, insurance, drugs, expenses, and luxuries—and she existed to cater to him and, for lack of a better term (and one he would never share with her), serve as his escort.

As far as Suzanne knew, Octavius's vast income came from the sale of his paintings and sculptures. It was actually humorous that his artwork had become nominally successful. Although Suzanne knew his income was supplemented by money he made from DoughWorx, the artisan bakery on the outskirts of Jessup, she had no clue that the entire upstairs of the business was dedicated to the illegal manufacture and distribution of synthetic opioids—mainly fentanyl mixed with cocaine. Jessup Mayor Marsden Maddox was in on the partnership, along with another power broker from Charleston, Timmy Kondore, and four of Octavius's drug-runner acquaintances from St. Augustine.

"Here we are, here we are." Octavius passed Suzanne's full-time residence—five-fifty-two—and escorted her to the next door down, five-fifty-four—the secret place.

"You passed it," she argued.

"We're going to the secret place for tonight."

"Why?" she said, slowing him down. "I want to sleep in my own bed."

"Don't whine, dear. Just bear with me, okay? I have my reasons."

Octavius keyed his way in, kicked the door shut, took her into the bedroom and got her seated upright on the bed. He put her legs up, took her hat off, and leaned her back into the big pillows. "I'll be right back. We're going to do some of the pink stuff, real quickly. I don't want any complaining."

"Noooooo," Suzanne moaned. "Not that . . . please, please."

Her voice faded as he made his way into the kitchen, into the upper cupboard, where he grabbed a small bottle of methadone. He quickly poured a generous amount of the pink liquid into a medicine cup. He added water from the tap, put the cap on, and shook.

Suzanne was experiencing opioid intoxication. It would've been impossible for her to be at the dinner that night. She'd been itching badly and wringing her hands. The Deetzes would've known immediately something was way wrong. Even now her speech was slurred, and her pupils were fully dilated.

Octavius hurried back into the bedroom with the methadone

concoction, hoping the dosage would settle Suzanne down and relieve any obvious craving symptoms.

"Oct-a-vi-ush," Suzanne slurred his name, "please don't make me take that. Have you tasted it? It's so bad. It's awful. I'll throw up!"

He almost laughed at her child-like speech, as he sat next to her and removed the top from the small cup. Her behavior reminded him of someone who'd just been gassed at the dentist's office. "Baby, this is going to make you feel more like yourself, okay? This way you'll be able to spend time with your friend, Joanie. Take this and—"

"No!" She shoved his hand, splashing some of the methadone onto his hand and pants.

His eyes lit up and he clenched one of her wrists as hard as he could with his free hand. She squirmed. Through clenched teeth he said, "You're *going* to take this. You know why? Cuz you got us into this *mess* with your friends the Deetzes, and you're going to sober up enough to get us out of it."

He didn't rely on methadone often, but Octavius knew it acted like a mild opioid while blocking any crazy withdrawal symptoms. It should have Suzanne evened out by morning so she would be coherent to meet with Joanie—one last time.

With the mess of the sticky pink medicine on his hands and leg, he eyed the cup, figuring there was still enough in it, and forced it to her lips. He pulled her hair back and forced her to drink it down. She did, but she instantly shot forward with a mortified expression —as if she'd just drank petroleum.

The doorbell from next door rang faintly through the thin walls.

Then Octavius heard knocking, also faint.

Wayne and Joanie were at Suzanne's place next door.

Octavius held a finger to his lips and got right up in Suzanne's face. "Shhh. Not a peep, beautiful. Not one peep." Suzanne was still reeling from the rotten taste of the methadone. She gagged and buried her head in the pillows like a spoiled brat.

Octavius got up and tiptoed back into the kitchen, even though he knew the Deetzes could not hear or see him. He washed his hands, wiped his pants with the damp towel, wiped off the methadone bottle, and returned it to the cupboard.

The doorbell next door rang faintly again followed by louder knocks this time.

Octavius walked softly to the window next to the door of the apartment. He probably shouldn't risk looking out, but he couldn't resist. Ever so gently, he lifted one of the slats in the blinds a tiny bit and peered over toward the door of Suzanne's apartment. The angle was such that he couldn't see the Deetzes standing at the door.

He heard the water running in the bathroom and hurried in to check on Suzanne. She glanced up at him as she was splashing water on her face. Then she scrubbed her hands vigorously with soap and water and dried off with a big towel.

"Your friends are next door." Octavius eyed her as he leaned in the doorway.

"What'd you expect?" She held the towel up to her cheeks and stared at him with mascara running beneath her eyes.

"I had no expectations. They're your friends."

"Joanie. Joanie is my friend." She looked at herself in the mirror. "We were going to spend time together." She stepped closer to the mirror, leaned over the sink, and examined her bloodshot eyes and dilated pupils in the reflection. Her brown hair was a staticky birds' nest. She really did look awful.

She began to cry.

"Shh, shh now." Octavius enveloped her in his big arms. "Don't cry."

She pounded his chest with a fist.

He embraced her tighter.

She then returned the embrace, sobbing. "What's happening?" she cried. "Those women—"

"Shh, shh, shh now." He squeezed her tight. "You were hallucinating again."

"No! No. Who were they?" she cried. "What is that place?"

She probably doesn't even know where it is.

"Come." He led her back into the bedroom. "Lay down."

"I don't want to." She pulled away, losing her balance, still clutching the towel. She headed into the living room. "Joanie's next door?" She swung around and glared at him, her nose dripping. She wiped it with the towel.

A complete mess.

He nodded. "They had dinner with me, at my place, remember? You weren't up to it. Joanie's been calling and texting you—"

Suzanne jerked as if shocked, then scanned the room. "Where's my phone?"

"Shhh. Keep your voice *down!*" he ordered. "I have your phone. Don't worry. You need to be quiet now. They've been wondering where you are. We'll let them leave for now. But tomorrow morning you should be in good enough shape to see Joanie. After that, how about we get really high, hmm? Go to euphoria land. How does that sound?"

He knew the opioids were her master. She'd do anything to continue riding that high. Just like the others.

"I feel bad about Joanie." She threw the towel over a chair and rubbed her nose and eyes deeply with her hands. Then she began scratching her neck and back, almost frantically.

"You've no reason to feel bad or to worry. They're on vacation. It's not all about you—"

"But they're here—now. They must think something's wrong."

Octavius tilted his head and shrugged. "What do you propose we do, go over there and tell them you've been high on opioids today and couldn't pull it together enough to have dinner? Hmm?" He approached her, his tone getting angrier with each step.

While we're at it we can tell them I manufacture the stuff.

Suzanne walked to the sliding glass doors and opened the curtains.

"Close that!" Octavius whispered loudly. "What're you thinking?"

She spun around, practically falling to the ground, but she kept her balance. "You're evil . . . you know that?"

He threw his head back and laughed quietly.

The fake laugh.

Because, in that instant, he knew she was right.

Ever since Father Pat's advances toward him when he was a boy, his life had spiraled into blackness. Now, at his age, there was no coming back. He'd been broken a long time ago. His only option, besides ending it, was to live each day for pleasure and nothing more, so hot in pursuit of the next adrenaline rush that he never had time to think about the monster he'd become.

He snapped himself out of it. "I get you what you need, Suzanne," he said. "It's that simple."

And then, you give me what I need. Just like the others.

"This is so messed up." She sat hard on the coffee table, like a drunk, and began to cry again.

"Stop it!" Octavius blasted. *"Enough."* He dug into his jacket, pulled out her phone, and jabbed it into her hands. "You're going to text Joanie—now."

Suzanne tried to get the phone to work, finally figured out it was off, and powered it up. The white apple appeared on the black screen.

"You're going to apologize profusely and say that, after the mechanic fixed your car, you got a call from a relative saying that your uncle or aunt or someone is dying and you've got to go there tomorrow; I don't care where, make something up."

"But—"

He spoke over her. "You're going to say that before you leave town you can grab breakfast with her—just the two of you. Set it up for 8 a.m., Cinnamon Shack. You're not asking her, you're telling her."

Octavius was afraid if Suzanne continued putting off meeting with Joanie, Deetz would continue sticking his detective nose way too far into their business. But if Suzanne could pull off the one simple, quick breakfast with Joanie, that would be the end of it. The Deetzes would understand she had a family emergency and would go on with their merry vacation, dropping out of his life—for good.

Octavius watched as Suzanne got the phone on and began to scroll through her text messages. A hand went to her mouth. She began seeing the missed calls and texts from Joanie, he assumed. She looked up at Octavius with her mouth gaping.

"You were on one of your binges, what can I say? If you want to keep getting your regular supply of oxy and you don't want to get busted you need to do what I just told you to do. Text her. Right now."

The doorbell and knocking next door had stopped. Octavius

wondered if the Deetzes had gone back to their little mousetrap. He hoped so.

"Do you remember what I told you to write?" he asked.

"Yes."

With that, Octavius returned to the window by the door and peeked through the blinds, but couldn't see anyone. He then walked into the bedroom, turned out the lights, crossed to the back window, and peered out—wondering if Deetz would be foolish enough to continue meddling where he didn't belong.

He heard Suzanne's phone ring in the other room and rushed to it.

Suzanne was sitting there on the coffee table, holding the ringing phone up in the air. "It's Joanie. I'm answering . . ."

"Don't you dare!"

11

Deetz had returned to the car and was sitting in the passenger seat next to Joanie. His hands and feet were still freezing, and he was trying not to show how disturbed he was at Suzanne's earlier condition—staggering inside—and that she and Octavius had somehow managed to go dark on them.

"She's still not answering," Joanie slapped her phone against her thigh. "We need to go around back—see if we can see anything."

"They'll have the curtains pulled," Deetz said. "They obviously don't want to be bothered."

"*He* doesn't want to be bothered. *She* looked like she needed help."

Deetz blew into his hands, rubbed them, and contemplated what to do. He knew Joanie wouldn't leave until they'd done all they could.

"Okay, let's go around back again." He opened his door. "Stay close to me."

The night air was crisp. Deetz could see Joanie's breath and a thousand stars in the black sky. As they made their way through the windy breezeway and down the hall toward the back of the apartments, he found it almost laughable that, here he was on vacation, doing police work. But he had to remember, he was a civilian now, not a cop. No badge. No gun.

They passed by the dark unit, the one with the Christmas tree, the one with the drapes drawn, and arrived at the rear of Suzanne's place. Deetz stopped and held up a hand for Joanie to do the same. He was puzzled.

"Come on." Joanie took a step closer to Suzanne's stone patio. "We can still see in."

"Hold up." Deetz grabbed her arm. He couldn't believe the curtain wasn't shut.

It looked exactly as it had when they'd checked the first time.

"You stay right here," he whispered. "I'll go up there."

Deetz surveyed the landscape to make sure no one was watching and quickly approached the stone patio and crossed to the sliding glass doors. The curtain was still open exactly as it had been. Oddly, nothing had changed inside—no other lights on, no keys on the table, not one thing had been moved.

No one's in there.

It made his mind go blank for a second.

What's going on?

He supposed it was possible Octavius had seen them in the parking lot, hid somewhere with Suzanne, and was waiting for them to leave.

Once again, he examined the still apartment. He supposed they could be hunkering down in a bedroom, but a light would be on or something would be different than when he had looked in earlier. His gut told him they weren't in there at all.

The only other option was that they had gone into another unit —which was highly unlikely and completely weird.

Deetz looked back at Joanie.

She was staring down at her glowing phone. After a second, her head shot up and she pointed dramatically at the screen.

He slashed at his throat, motioning for her to dowse the bright light, and headed toward where she was standing.

"It's from Suzanne." She handed him the phone.

He reduced the brightness and read the text message: "So sorry to miss dinner friend. Car fixed but I just got word my uncle had a heart attack. I've got to go to Bend. I can meet for breakfast before I cut out. 8am Cinnamon Shack in Sedona. See you there. I'm beat. Turning off phone for the night."

Deetz handed Joanie the phone. "Let's go back to the car." He started walking.

"Wayne!" Joanie whispered.

He turned back to Joanie, who was staring at the apartment next to Suzanne's. With her mouth barely moving she whispered, "Someone's looking out."

Just as Deetz set eyes on the back window of the apartment next to Suzanne's, a two-inch opening in the blinds dropped shut.

∽

"There was a light on in that room before," Joanie said.

"Back to the car, come on." Deetz took her arm and started walking briskly toward the parking lot.

"What's going on, Wayne?"

"We'll talk in the car."

Octavius's Mercedes and Suzanne's white Kia were still in the parking lot.

They got back into the rental and Wayne locked the doors, started it, and cranked up the heat.

"I should call her," Joanie said.

"The text said she was turning it off. She—or they—don't want you to contact her. She won't answer."

"Why was she staggering? Where were they coming from?" Joanie insisted. "None of it makes sense. Why is he even here?"

"I wonder if she even had car trouble?" Wayne said. "If I could see under the hood of her car I might be able to tell if the alternator's new."

"I'm worried," Joanie said.

"It's definitely weird."

"We need to stay here and watch what he does next," Joanie said.

Wayne looked at his watch.

"We could sit here forever, honey," he said. "He may spend the night here—wherever they are."

She knew it was getting late, but she didn't care. "Or something else crazy could happen. We can't leave, Wayne."

"She's going to meet you for breakfast. Let's head back for now."

"He could have texted that, not her. He probably did!"

"Hold up, hold up." Wayne's voice got dead serious. He was staring toward the entrance of Suzanne's building. "Oh boy."

It was Octavius. He was walking out, alone, heading for his car.

"Oh my gosh." Chills engulfed Joanie's arms.

The Mercedes beeped, its lights flashed, and Octavius approached the driver's door.

But, suddenly, he lifted his head and looked directly at Wayne and Joanie, and stared into their car for a good five seconds. Then his head tilted in surprise and recognition.

"Uh-oh," Wayne said through closed mouth.

Octavius began walking straight toward them.

"Go Wayne, go!"

"Too late now." Wayne sat frozen, staring straight at the tall man as he approached Joanie's side of the car in a jovial manner.

"Put your window down," Wayne said in monotone.

Joanie scrambled to find the button, her hands shaking and heart pounding.

Finally, she found it and the window buzzed down.

"What're you folks doing here?" Octavius bent over and looked in at them, the whites of his eyes clear and glistening in the cold night air.

Joanie tried to fake a laugh and started to make something up, but Wayne spoke first.

"Joanie got worried. Suzanne wasn't responding to any of her calls or texts, so we decided to run over."

An awkward silence hung in the air.

"I rang the bell and knocked a few minutes ago," Deetz continued. "Did you guys hear me?"

"Yes, yes . . . sorry about that." Octavius stuffed his hands in his coat pockets and looked back and forth at them as he spoke. "I couldn't get to the door." He let out a huff and his breath steamed into the air. "The second you left StoneSpell, she called back, distraught . . . her uncle had a heart attack tonight—back in Bend. She's very close to him, like the father she never had. Anyway, he's not doing well—might not make it."

"That's awful," Joanie said.

Octavius paused awkwardly as if figuring out what to say next. "When she got the news she decided it was too late to fly out tonight." He looked around the parking lot. "She actually Ubered over to Reggie's, one of our local haunts, and drowned her sorrows. In the process, she had one too many martinis."

That did not sound at all like the Suzanne who Joanie knew.

"I kept tabs on her, and it sounded like she needed a hand getting tucked in." Octavius chuckled. "So, I ran over and brought her back. She's fine now. Nothing to worry about. She was sound asleep even before I left."

Joanie and Wayne both seemed to be speechless.

Octavius sighed loudly again, stood up and stepped back several feet from the car. "She's going to fly out tomorrow, so I don't know if I'll see you guys again. It's been amazing to meet you both."

"She texted me and said she wants to have breakfast before she leaves," Joanie said.

"Oh really?" Octavius said. "What time? I hope it's early, because I need to get her to the airport."

"Eight," Joanie said.

"Oh, wow!" Octavius snickered. "She probably didn't realize when she texted you the size of hangover she's going to have that early in the morning. Bear with her, Joanie, I can assure you she's not going to be firing on all cylinders at that hour."

Joanie and Wayne both stared at him.

"I may even give her a wakeup call—just to make sure she doesn't stand you up!"

"It's good to have met you," Wayne said. "Thank you again for dinner."

"Yes, it was very nice," Joanie said.

"It was my pleasure, indeed." Octavius waved and began walking back to his car. "Next time, Joanie, we'll go on that hike!"

12

Suzanne was awakened by the sound of the coffee maker gurgling in the kitchen. She kept her eyes closed and pulled the blankets tight around her and up close to her chin. Her head floated and her throat was parched. She needed a drink of water and to go to the bathroom, but she wasn't going anywhere yet.

More sleep.

The coffee maker continued its final spitting and spurting. She wondered what Octavius was doing there so early? She squinted for her bedside clock, but it wasn't there. *That's right.* She was in the secret place, next door to her apartment. She rolled over with a groan and peeked toward the nightstand on the other side of the bed, knowing there was a clock there: 6:45 a.m.

The room was still dark, no light coming in around the window. She closed her eyes and snuggled in, trying to get back to sleep.

But her foggy mind began to work.

She'd missed the dinner with Joanie and Wayne.

Her face flushed.

How could you do that?

Octavius had brought her back there in a huff the night before and had made her drink the awful pink stuff, which still coated her tongue and throat. As she flipped restlessly in the big bed, the base of her throat burned with nausea—a side effect to which she'd grown accustomed.

As she remembered that Joanie and Wayne had come to her apartment the night before, looking for her, she became alarmed.

They're going to think something is seriously wrong. And Wayne is a cop.

Octavius had made her text Joanie . . .

Breakfast!

8 a.m.

Suzanne's eyes flicked open.

She instantly began to sweat.

Her breathing tightened.

She rocketed up to a sitting position on the side of the bed realizing she was wearing Octavius's huge black boxers and enormous white T-shirt.

Her heart hammered and she couldn't get a deep breath.

She remembered the dark room at StoneSpell—with the beds, and the two other women.

A light turned on beneath the door and she heard the shower go on in the adjacent bathroom.

She began to gasp for air.

Stay calm, stay calm!

She wanted to go to Octavius, but she was frozen, concentrating on getting her next breath.

Relax. Relax. Relax.

The bedroom door opened and Octavius's tall silhouette filled the doorframe. He realized she was having a panic attack and was instantly beside her, rocking her, running a hand through her hair, assuring her everything was okay.

Gradually, Suzanne's breathing calmed and the sweat on her body turned freezing cold. Her left leg bounced at a hundred miles an hour.

Noticing that her teeth were chattering, Octavius brought the big blanket up around her shoulders. "Better?" he said.

She nodded just to get him to shut up.

Something was bad wrong and she knew it.

She knew it was the opioids. They *owned* her. And, for that reason, *he* owned her. But she *needed* the drugs. In fact, as much as she tried, she couldn't fathom life without them. Hadn't wanted to.

"Come on, now." He stood and helped her up. "Let's get you a nice hot shower, then we'll get you a little bump before you meet Joanie—"

"Little?" she snapped.

"Little, for now." He nodded as he got her into the steamy bathroom. "Once you're done with your friend, we'll sneak off and get really jammed—okay? That sound good?"

She was glad the mirror was foggy, because she knew she looked like a train wreck.

"Leave me." She filled a glass with cold water and drank it down, spilling a lot down her chin.

"Want coffee?" he said.

"Yes."

He gave her a peck on the cheek, walked out, and closed the door.

Does he really care about me?

Why is he attracted to me when I look like this?

Suzanne cleared a spot on the mirror with a wash cloth, leaned over the sink, and examined her face. She was right, she looked like she'd slept in a box in an alley. Her hair was a nasty bird's nest. Her eyes were watery and her pupils were so large she could barely see the blue of her eyes. She had a raw patch the size of a dime beneath her left eye from scratching it so badly.

She couldn't look any longer.

She stripped and got in the shower, almost losing her balance.

The water she'd drank sat uneasy in her stomach and her upper chest burned again with nausea.

As the hot water pelted her face, head, and back, Suzanne knew she should care more about Joanie, about spending time with her during their visit—as she'd promised. She'd had all kinds of high hopes about showing them all the sights, cooking for them, spending time talking about old times.

But the ugly truth was, she couldn't care less about any of that now. She didn't even want to see Joanie for breakfast. She just wanted her next hit.

As she reached down for the bottle of shampoo, she had to steady herself, and she realized how slowly she was moving. It wasn't normal. She knew the drugs were taking a toxic toll on her body and mind. But she didn't care, because nothing, *nothing* made her feel like what Octavius provided for her. It was beyond description.

She realized she would need to do a bang up job on her makeup before meeting Joanie, and she certainly wasn't going to sit around there long. She was already anxious to meet back up with Octavius and was craving whatever he had to give her. Somehow, he always knew exactly what would take her away to that place of complete relaxation. Some days it was oxycodone, other days it was codeine or hydrocodone. She didn't care what it was called. He knew how to administer it safely. She trusted him. Most of it was pills, some of it they smoked. He'd talked about shooting heroin, but she'd told him no—although she might be able to be persuaded.

She heard the door of the bathroom open.

"Coffee, madam." Octavius pulled open the shower curtain and grinned.

"Hey!" she screamed.

"Don't you want a sip?" He held up the brown coffee cup with both hands.

She reached up and jerked the shower curtain closed. "Just leave it."

"Aren't we testy this morning?" he said.

"You know what I need," she yelled.

"What if I told you it's in the coffee?" he said.

Suzanne contemplated his words for a few foggy seconds, then ripped the curtain open.

Octavius threw his head back and laughed, holding the cup out to her again.

She stared at the cup and reached out with trembling hands, as if reaching for a bowl of diamonds.

She sipped at first, to make sure it wasn't too hot. He'd added cream and sugar. It was perfect.

"Go on, now," she told him. "I need my privacy."

"Not even a thank you?" he said.

"Thank you. Now go."

Octavius shrugged as he walked out the door.

Suzanne stood there dripping, half in and half out of the shower, savoring every swig of the drug cocktail—until it was gone.

"Ahh."

She set the cup on the sink and got back in the shower.

As she shampooed her hair, she could sense the drug kicking in, because suddenly everything was okay again. Her mind gradually lifted to that higher plane where there were no worries. She completely relaxed and focused on finishing the shower and drying off. No hair dryer, no big deal—she towel-dried it.

Wiping a large portion of the mirror, she noticed red scratches at all angles on her stomach and arms; she turned to look at her back and they were there, too. That was one of the side effects, but she gladly lived with it, as well as periodic insomnia. What was a little scratching and sleeplessness when she could live carefree, not worried about anything—not thinking ahead about anything? Just gliding along in the moment, almost above everything, not thinking deeply about anything? Besides, these were pain-killers she was on, so she didn't notice the scratches, or any physical pain for that matter.

She did her make-up, covering the itchy patch beneath her eye as best she could. Then she got dressed, choosing from the few outfits she had in the closet at the secret place. It was all fine.

Entering the kitchen where Octavius hovered over a huge pan of scrambled eggs and cheese, the smell filled her senses.

"Ready?" he said.

"Yeah. I hope that's not for me."

"Nope. I'm starved," he said, scraping the eggs onto a big plate. "Let's talk about what you're going to say to Joanie."

"I got it, okay? No need to give me a play-by-play." That was one thing about being on opioids, when someone forced her to face reality, it was war.

Standing at the counter, Octavius took a huge bite of the eggs and spoke with a mouthful. "I just want to make sure you don't talk about my past, really anything about me. Talk about the old days in Bend, but keep it short. Remember, your uncle had a heart attack in Bend. He's the father you never had. He's in serious condition. It was too late to fly out last night. You Ubered to Reggie's and had too many martinis—"

"She won't buy that."

"It's all I could think of, okay? I picked you up and brought you back here."

"But we weren't in my real apartment," she said.

"They don't know that. Don't worry about that. Just tell her I'm taking you to the airport soon and that's it. I'll pick you up and we'll go celebrate somewhere. I'll have the good stuff. Okay?"

"Yep."

"That's my girl."

13

Joanie was feeling weirdly anxious about her breakfast with Suzanne, and Wayne even commented about how quiet she'd been on the drive over as he turned off of 89A into one of Sedona's many touristy, high-end plazas.

"It's just awkward after she missed dinner last night," Joanie said as Deetz parked the car. "And then that whole thing at her place last night. I barely slept."

"Well, she's the one with all the explaining to do, not you. It's definitely going to be interesting. Wish I could join you," Wayne said.

"I wish you could go in my place." Joanie opened her door and got out.

"Take as long as you want, I'll find stuff to do." Wayne waved goodbye and pulled away. He had his rental bike in the back of the SUV and was on his way to the bike shop to get the brakes looked at because he couldn't get them to stop squeaking.

It was a cold morning, in the thirties, but the sun was shining on the Red Rock Mountains in the distance. The Cinnamon Shack looked to be one of the few businesses open yet in the fancy two-story plaza, which was packed with all kinds of businesses—an art gallery, a cantina, several clothing stores, an ice cream shop, something about a crystal vortex, and an aroma healing center.

Joanie didn't see Suzanne's car. She went in. Bells tinkled and an older woman with a pleasant smile and dyed black hair took her to a small booth next to the window, which was wet with condensation. She handed Joanie a laminated menu and Joanie noticed a tattoo of a German shepherd on the woman's outstretched arm.

Joanie told her she was expecting someone so the waitress left a second menu and turned over both cups. At Joanie's request, the waitress disappeared and hurried back with a carafe of coffee and poured Joanie a cup.

Joanie sipped the coffee and was immediately disappointed. It was warm, not hot, and miserably weak. She glanced at the menu, hoping the breakfast wouldn't be equally as disappointing.

Movement caught her eye outside and sure enough it was Octavius's big shiny Mercedes, which swung into the parking lot very quickly and came to an abrupt halt, taking up three parking spaces. Octavius turned toward Suzanne and talked to her in what appeared to be an authoritative way, as if giving her instructions.

Suzanne threw up her hands nonchalantly, opened the door, and got out. She wore large sunglasses, a thick beige fleece coat, expensive jeans and brown leather boots. She spotted Joanie in the window, waved and made her way inside. Octavius zipped off.

Joanie stood and they hugged then sat down.

"Well you sure had a rough day yesterday," Joanie said. "Sorry to hear about your uncle."

The waitress whisked in and filled Suzanne's coffee cup.

"Don't even get me started. It was a nightmare. I'm so sorry I missed dinner. I feel awful," Suzanne said. "I hope Octavius kept you entertained."

"Oh . . . he did, he did. The dinner was incredible. He made Thai food. And his place is amazing. That back deck area is to die for."

"Isn't it? Did you do the hot tub?"

"Oh no," Joanie laughed shyly. "But he put the fire on. He showed me his sculpture."

"Which one?"

"Uhh . . . Venus." She was embarrassed to even say it.

"Oh yeah, she's something, isn't she?" Suzanne laughed and sipped her coffee, not seeming bothered by how weak it was. "He's got others on the property, too. Isn't he talented? So, he wasn't too overpowering for you?"

Actually, he was awkwardly overpowering.

"Oh, he's very . . . charismatic," Joanie said.

"That's a good word for him. So, how do you like Sedona?"

Joanie wasn't about to say she could never live there.

"Good. We've been doing a lot of biking and hiking. I'm just sorry you're going to have to leave. Bummer."

Suzanne nodded and looked down at her coffee. "I know. I'm sorry. This uncle is really close. Uncle Steve. You met him, didn't you, when we were kids?"

"Is he the one who brought those two huge jars of homemade pickles to one of your family picnics."

"That's the one!"

They both laughed.

"You remember the situation with my Dad and Mom? Why they separated?" Suzanne said.

"Your dad traveled all the time. Wasn't that the crux of it?"

Suzanne nodded. "He was gone Monday through Friday. We found out later about all his affairs. They divorced."

"I know, I remember. How's your dear Mom doing, anyway? I miss old Barbara. I haven't seen her in so long."

"She's actually great. She went on without missing a beat. She has a ton of friends. She's in a walking group, a gardening club. Has a good church. She's strong. And she's happy."

"I always loved her," Joanie said.

"So, Uncle Steve came on the scene after the divorce. He's my Mom's brother. He never had kids. He kind of took me under his wing when Dad left. He was there for all the big stuff."

"So he had a heart attack?" Joanie noticed Suzanne hadn't removed her sunglasses or coat.

"Yeah. Really serious. He might not make it." She looked at her watch. "I can't stay long."

"Should we order some food?" Joanie said, feeling rushed.

"You go ahead. I'm good."

"You've got to eat something before you travel. Come on, let's just get a quick bite."

"Okay." Suzanne looked at her menu. "They're known for their cinnamon sticky buns." Suzanne raised a hand for the waitress, who saw her and came over.

Joanie did a double take because she'd barely glanced at the menu.

"Sorry about that," Suzanne said. "Are you ready?"

"I can be," Joanie said, still scanning the menu.

"I'll have a sticky bun, please; extra napkins," Suzanne said.

The waitress looked at Joanie. "And for you?"

"I'll go with the number one, traditional breakfast. Over easy. Bacon."

"Wow, you wouldn't know you ate like that. You look amazing," Suzanne said.

"It's vacation. We're splurging."

"Wayne looks good, too."

"We both work hard at it."

They sipped their coffee over an awkward silence.

"So, you mentioned you're not working?" Joanie said.

Suzanne shook her head and looked down again. "I did the real estate thing for a while, but I was just sick of it, you know? You get to be our age—I'm tired of working."

"How do you support yourself?" Joanie said, not caring how personal a question it was.

Suzanne hesitated. "I've got money in savings. My investments have done well. And I'll get my social security in a couple more years. I don't need a lot to live on. Plus, Octavius treats me to everything. He takes really good care of me."

"Will you two get married, do you think?"

Suzanne leaned back and laughed. "I'd marry him today if he asked me, but he's very . . . nontraditional. I'm just not sure. We'll see."

"So, what do you guys do for fun?" Joanie said.

"Oh man. Well, let's see. He's turned me on to yoga and meditation, which has been amazing. There's something absolutely magical about the Red Rocks. Like, there's a force here—a connection you make, with yourself. If you want to find it, it's there. I've never experienced anything like it before."

Joanie was glad Wayne wasn't there. He would have rolled his eyes and said something extremely obnoxious.

"Octavius is super busy at his studio, plus he has a side business—it's an artisan bread company."

"Oh, yeah. He told us about that. We want to go."

"You must."

"And what about church?" Joanie said. "Are you going?"

Suzanne looked out the window in a daze. "I haven't been. I know it sounds awful, but to be honest, this focus on nourishing my conscious mind and radical self-care has done more for me than church ever did."

Joanie knew self-care was a hot topic these days, but she was saddened because it sounded as if Suzanne had used that to replace her relationship with God.

"Nothing against the church," Suzanne said. "But when I look at Freddie—" She shook her head sharply, mumbled something, and snickered. "Sorry, Octavius. Rough night last night. But his life is just so care-free and spontaneous. He lives each day to the fullest."

Joanie made a mental note of the 'Freddie' slip up.

Suzanne rambled on. "Octavius has shown me what it's like to feel safe being myself, to live in my bliss. He's studied the healing arts, so he knows how to—this'll sound weird to you—but we create our own personal altars."

Oh great.

Joanie had heard enough on that topic. "You called him Freddie. Is that a nickname?"

"Oh, yeah in fact it is." Suzanne smiled and looked out the window. "He bumped into an old friend at the Red Rocks Music Festival; it's this great annual thing they do with chamber music and solo concerts. Anyway, the guy recognized him and called out, 'Freddie!' And I thought, 'Wrong guy, dude.' But Octavius told me later that was his nickname growing up."

"So, where did you guys meet?" Joanie said.

"Oh, it's the funniest story. I'd just had a tooth pulled two days before, so my jaw was bruised and swollen and I was an absolute mess, groggy on pain meds, but I had to get out for some air. I'd been resting for two days. So, there was this art show in town—"

"In Jessup?" Joanie said.

"Yes. And Octavius had a big booth in the show. So, I wandered into his booth, all bruised, swollen, looking like a hag—and I just fell in love with his paintings. I mean I was mesmerized. Looking back, I wonder if it was the pain meds I was on." She laughed. "But anyway, he finally came over and we got into this *deep* conversation. He was like hypnotizing. He swept me off my feet with his positive energy."

Okay, this is too much.

Joanie forced a smile and nodded.

Thank goodness, the waitress stepped in with their plates and refilled their coffees. Joanie silently thanked God for the food and asked him to give her wisdom with Suzanne.

"Anyway, he ended up *giving me* the painting I was fawning over," Suzanne continued as she picked up her sticky bun and took a bite. "He had me charmed from the instant I met him."

"It's amazing how successful he's become as an artist in such a short time," Joanie said. "Did he do art before, in St. Augustine?"

"He's always painted. But he came here specifically to give it a go full-time. He scouted cities all over the U.S. So he hand-picked the Sedona area, because it's such an incredible arts community."

They both ate. Joanie's food wasn't very hot and was just average. Suzanne devoured her sticky bun, licking her fingers with each bite, sunglasses still on.

"How long was he in St. Augustine?" Joanie said.

"Not sure. He's lived a lot of different places."

"He was in boat sales?"

"Yeah. We actually went back there together once." Suzanne laughed and wiped her mouth with her napkin. "It was crazy. We drove a boat, a huge yacht, from St. Augustine up to Charleston—as in Charleston, South Carolina! Oh my goodness, the sky turned black. We got into a storm and hit the roughest water, like six-foot waves. Octavius didn't have that much experience driving a boat. I got sick. I thought we were going to flip. I wanted to call the Coast Guard, but he refused. He insisted on plowing through. I'll never do that again."

"What was in Charleston?"

"We delivered the yacht to this filthy rich guy who had a mansion right at the port, on Sullivan's Island. Incredible. Turns out the guy was best friends with the mayor of Jessup, Marsden Maddox, who we've become great friends with—he and his wife Candace."

Joanie took mental notes, concentrating hard to remember everything.

"What was his name?" Joanie said.

"Who?" Suzanne said, looking suddenly annoyed.

"The guy who bought the boat."

Suzanne shrugged. "Kondore. Timmy Kondore."

"So, Octavius was still in the boat business when he came to Jessup?"

Suzanne dug a compact out of her purse. "Kind of." She re-applied her lipstick. "It was a last deal he had to wrap up—something like that."

Suzanne checked her phone. She read a text and began texting back. "Okay, he's coming to get me soon." She finished typing and looked up at Joanie. "He's always like three hours early to the airport. We haven't got to talk about you. Do you think there's any way you'll retire here?"

Joanie knew there wasn't but didn't want to send a negative vibe.

"Not sure yet. I think we're going to start doing this more—visiting potential retirement spots. We want to check out Asheville in North Carolina. We're sick of Portland; it's a mess. Downtown's ruined. Although, the boys will probably stay there, so we're not sure what we'll do. Wayne's got to decide whether he wants to retire now or work another year."

"Yeah, I remember you said that. He's been through a lot with those shootings—and Leena! I can't believe she got kidnapped. Is she okay?"

"You wouldn't even know it happened," Joanie said. "In fact, she thinks she's a big celebrity now."

They laughed, which felt good, but Joanie was concerned for Suzanne. Octavius just wasn't sitting well with her. The bottom line was that his influence had pulled her away from God.

What does light have in common with darkness?

Suzanne inquired about the boys and Joanie caught her up quickly on each of them, but she felt beholden to inquire more about her wellbeing.

"So, how are you doing spiritually?" Joanie said. "Everything good?"

Suzanne looked up quickly toward the parking lot. "Oops, there he is." She worked her way out of the booth.

She can't wait to get out of here!

Joanie got out, too. They gave a quick hug.

"Sorry we won't get to see more of you," Joanie said. "Hope your uncle is okay."

Suzanne set two twenties on the table. "This is my treat."

Joanie began to object, then a horn sounded from the parking lot. It was Octavius, who had parked at the curb right out front, next to the 'No Parking' sign.

Suzanne shook her head and rolled her eyes. "Sorry about that." She began backing toward the door. "He doesn't want me to miss this flight."

For someone who's so 'carefree and spontaneous,' Octavius sure was uptight.

"Good luck, okay?" Joanie said, feeling totally disappointed with the visit. "Let's keep in touch."

"We will. Maybe you can come back again, and we can do this right next time." Suzanne called out as she got to the door. "Or, I'll come to Portland!"

Joanie didn't believe for a second that Suzanne really wanted to do either.

The horn honked again—longer this time.

And Suzanne was gone.

14

The instant Suzanne's car door shut Octavius gunned the Mercedes throwing her back in her seat. The car whizzed through the parking lot and bounced onto the street as he turned left and planned to head out of town. "How'd it go?" he said.

"You could have given us more time," Suzanne said.

"Just being cautious. The longer you stayed the more apt you'd have been to say something you shouldn't."

"Where are we headed?" Suzanne sounded annoyed. She looked straight ahead.

Octavius could always tell when she needed the next bump—she became extremely belligerent.

"You didn't say anything you shouldn't, did you?" he said.

"Of course not," she said, angrily. "You make it sound so . . . criminal. We're not doing anything *that* bad. My gosh, get over it."

"No. Of course not," he shot back. "Just call me paranoid. He's just a cop and you're taking opioids—illegally."

Octavius could sense Suzanne staring at him now as he merged onto the freeway.

"You make it sound pretty bad," she said. "If it's that bad, why do you give it to me?"

Because you can't live without it—and it keeps you in your place.

"It would be bad if I got caught, but I'm not planning on that happening," Octavius said. "That's why I wanted to get you away from her as swiftly as possible."

"You act like I'm a child."

Because that's exactly what you are.

He said nothing and increased his speed. Driving the Benz on the highway was like riding on air; seventy-five felt like twenty-five. He'd been summoned rather urgently to a meeting by his business associates, Mayor Marsden Maddox and Charleston business magnate Timmy Kondore, at their DoughWorx location outside Jessup.

"What do you have for me?" Suzanne stuck her hand out.

Octavius stuffed a hand in his coat pocket and handed her two oblong white pills, each containing a combination of two pain relievers: 5mg hydrocodone and 325mg acetaminophen.

Suzanne glared at him with the pills in her outstretched hand, as if waiting for more.

"That's it for now," he said. "More soon."

Without thanking him, Suzanne threw the pills in her mouth, opened the plastic bottle of water from the console between them, and gulped them down.

For a patient recovering from surgery, one of the pills every four to six hours would be the doctor recommended dosage. But for Suzanne, two pills had become like candy. It often surprised Octavius what a tolerance she'd built up.

"Where're we going?" she asked again.

"DoughWorx. Then I thought we might go to The Wedgewood." He looked at her, waiting for her to light up. The Wedgewood was her favorite exclusive luxury spa—$600 a night.

"Hmm." Suzanne's eyebrows went up and down, but that was it.

"I thought you'd be more excited," he said.

"What's at DoughWorx?"

"Quick meeting—with Mars and Timmy."

Suzanne had no clue the three men manufactured and distributed their own opioids from the top floor of DoughWorx. As far as she knew, they were three-way owners in the artisan bread company and that was the extent of it.

Even Octavius didn't know why Mars had called the last-minute meeting, but he'd sounded uncharacteristically uptight.

"Where do you go . . . the nights you disappear?" Suzanne said, out of nowhere.

Octavius gulped, but remained silent. He wondered why the hydrocodone wasn't kicking in faster? It always hit her bloodstream rapidly and set her immediately at ease.

"Huh? Where do you go those nights?" Suzanne had removed her sunglasses and was rubbing beneath her left eye.

Octavius reached over and gently touched her wrist. "You're going to make that worse. Stop, before it bleeds."

She stopped abruptly and put her sunglasses back on. "Answer me."

He paused and told himself to remain calm. "Sometimes Mars and I meet up, sometimes I work late at the studio, sometimes I just need alone time," he said. "You don't want to be together every night, do you?"

"Are there other women?"

He looked over and she was staring at him, laser-focused.

Something's wrong. She's never serious after popping two loads.

"Of course not." He reached over with his right hand and covered both of hers, wondering what was going on.

"I think there are." She pulled her hands away. "And I think there's something really strange going on."

Alarms reverberated in his chest and he felt his face grow hot.

She must have been coherent enough to have seen the other women the night before, possibly even talked to them.

His insides churned. He was angry and distraught, but was determined to play it cool.

"Honey, now you've been a little off-schedule with your meds lately because Joanie and Wayne have been here," he said as if talking to a child. "I had to give you that methadone. We've been all out of sync. That's why I booked The Wedgewood, so we can get away, relax, sit in the sauna, get massages—get back on schedule. Hmm?"

She muttered something and looked out the passenger window.

Colorful hot air balloons dotted the horizon.

"Wow, look at those," he said, to get her off the topic. "Maybe we could do that someday?"

She continued staring out at them in silence.

Octavius leaned back, took a deep breath, and exhaled.

He glanced at her again. She was still looking out.

To sum things up, Suzanne was fun. She was pretty—although a bit chubby around the waist. She talked a bit too much and could be excessively immature at times, which was embarrassing around the class of people in whose circles he traveled. When she was high though, she gave him what he wanted; in fact, she scored quite high in that department. But that was the extent of it. There was nothing deeper than that.

Perhaps we've had our run.

Octavius was getting a bit tired of having someone on a leash, anyway. He liked his freedom.

Suzanne turned her head and looked straight ahead again. Tears streaked her face.

Hmm.

Octavius let up on the gas as he approached the exit for DoughWorx.

What is going on in her head?

He wasn't a mind-reader, but he knew one thing—no one was going to get in the way of the empire he was building.

No one.

15

As Deetz eased to a stop and parked the SUV in the plaza where he was picking up Joanie, he spotted her seated on a bench at the end of the parking lot where she had a nice view of the stark Red Rock Mountains. It was still cold, but the sun was rising in the east and she was soaking it in. He felt sorry for her—that she wouldn't get to see Suzanne anymore. That had been one of the main reasons they'd picked Sedona for their getaway.

Deetz got out and walked toward her. His skull still felt somewhat fragile from the concussion. From twenty feet away he gave a yell, "Hey pretty lady."

Joanie turned around. "Oh, hey there. That was fast."

"At your service."

"Want to sit a minute?"

"Yes . . . Wow." He went around and eased down next to her on the bench and put an arm around her. "What a view. Ahh, that sun feels good."

"You relaxed yet?"

"Getting there," he said.

"Get the bike fixed?"

"He said he'll get to it right away. I have to go back when he texts me . . . *if* he texts me. I have my doubts. It didn't look real organized in there."

"Ha."

"I looked for souvenirs for Leena and Brandon in some huge tourist trap and just ended up wandering like a zombie."

"Find anything?"

"Nothing but junk. I think those T-shirts we saw at that one outdoor stand may be our best bet."

"Wayne, those were cheap. And Leena doesn't wear T-shirts."

"Hmm. Maybe we'll take them each a magic, mystical rock from the magic, mystical mountains." He exaggerated the words to sound like a magician. "They can have a séance with them."

"I'm glad you weren't at breakfast. Suzanne was talking some weird stuff."

"Like what?"

Joanie's head swiveled and she looked at Wayne. "She doesn't go to church anymore. Instead, she 'feeds her conscious mind' and does 'radical self-care.' I mean, man has she changed."

"Oh boy."

"Yeah, she said Octavius is 'carefree and spontaneous,' more so than anyone she's ever met in church."

"Oh brother. He's doing a number on her."

"Yeah, now she 'lives in her bliss—'"

"You're kidding me right now."

Joanie shook her head. "I wish I was. Do you know what she said? Octavius has studied the healing arts and they create their own 'personal altars.'"

Deetz closed his eyes and sighed. He felt most sorry for Joanie.

Joanie got a tissue from her purse and wiped her nose.

Deetz patted her gently on the back in silence.

"We had so little time," Joanie blurted. "It was like he was rushing her to get breakfast over with. And she's not the same person. I mean, she literally seems like a different person than the one I knew."

"People change, honey," he said softly.

"Yeah, but people change people, too. You become like who you hang out with."

"Do you think she's happy?"

"What bothers me most is, she used to love God so much. She always challenged me. She inspired me to love God and to love others. Now it's all about worshipping herself—and Octavius."

Joanie blew her nose, stuffed the tissue in her purse, and said, "Listen to this." She unfolded a napkin from the restaurant on which she'd written something in black ink after Suzanne had left. "Freddie. She slipped at one point and called Octavius, Freddie. I asked her about it. He told her that was his old nickname. I need to get to a laptop. Something's not right about his past."

"You can do it on your phone."

"I need the laptop. My phone screen's too small," she said, still looking at the napkin. "Listen to this. Suzanne went with Octavius back to St. Augustine and they drove a yacht up to Charleston—in the Atlantic! She said Octavius was, I don't know, maybe making one last boat delivery for his old company? But why would he do that if he'd left the company?"

"When was this?"

"I don't know. I'm guessing a year or two ago," Joanie said. "Anyway, they delivered the yacht to this rich guy's mansion at the port of Charleston—Kondore's his name. Turns out he's friends with the mayor of Jessup, Marsden Maddox, who's good friends with Octavius and Suzanne."

Deetz was slowly growing frustrated with the whole Suzanne-Octavius saga. He shook his head. "But, all that's fine. People know people. I think maybe it's time to drop this whole thing. Can we just forget it and enjoy ourselves?"

Joanie put the napkin in the purse on her lap, leaned over the bag and sighed. "I care about her."

"I understand. But she's an adult and she's making her own decisions."

"I just wish I had more time with her."

In his own mind, Deetz was glad Suzanne was leaving town. She was proving toxic, upsetting Joanie, and ruining her vacation.

Deetz stood and took Joanie's cold hand. "What do you say I take you out to the fanciest restaurant in Sedona tonight?"

Joanie squeezed his hand, stood, and tried to give him a smile through her frown. "Sounds good."

"Sounds good? Good!" Deetz began walking to the car, swinging Joanie's arm, trying to get her to laugh. "There's a place I've researched . . . it's off the beaten path, only the locals know about it. It's called The Mainstay. They're specialty is—drum roll please . . . lamb adobo."

Joanie snickered, took Deetz's arm, and snuggled close as they walked. "I love you," she whispered.

"I love you," he said.

"You should call the bike shop so we can pick it up on the way back, hopefully," Joanie said.

"Great minds think alike."

They got into the car and Deetz dialed the number for the bike shop, while Joanie stared at the restaurant window where she'd sat with Suzanne.

After decades of marriage, Deetz knew Joanie almost as well as he knew himself. As the phone for the bike shop rang over the car speaker and Joanie continued staring at the Cinnamon Shack, Deetz knew one thing for sure—she wasn't done investigating Octavius Hunt.

16

Octavius had wanted Suzanne to wait in the car at DoughWorx during his meeting with the partners, but she'd insisted on venturing inside; she said she had a book to read on her phone and wanted more coffee.

As usual, Octavius nodded and waved to various well-wishers who recognized him as the owner, and as the gregarious painter from the popular art studio in Jessup. Gracefully, he got Suzanne seated at a cozy leather couch by the blazing gas log fireplace, feeling the eyes of the locals upon him, and again wishing Suzanne hadn't wanted to tag along.

Fifteen to twenty people were scattered about in the spacious café portion of the artisan bread company, which was designed with low lighting and comfy seating—a cross between a Starbucks and a high-end lodge at a ski resort. It was quiet and comfortable, with an upbeat vibe. Many patrons were regulars who came each morning for coffee and for the bakery's famous DoughKnots, a tangled delight of mouthwatering pastry and cranberries with a warm, sugary glaze that included almonds, walnuts, and powdered sugar.

Octavius went through the swinging door to get behind the counter. He poured a coffee for Suzanne, grabbed her a DoughKnot from the fresh tray in the glass showcase, delivered it to her with excess kindness for the onlookers, and returned to pour himself a coffee.

"Good morning, Tate, has anyone arrived for me?" Octavius spoke to the tall, gray-bearded chef, who wore a smudged white apron and tall white baker's hat.

"Yes, sir. They are in the executive suite." Tate's features always reminded Octavius of the famous Van Gogh self-portrait. He was rough around the edges but had always been a top employee.

"Did you serve them?" Octavius said.

"Yes, sir. They are taken care of."

Octavius patted the bony man on the back. "Good man, Tate. Thank you. Listen, when you get a chance either wash that hat or get a new one."

Tate just stared at him, evenly.

Octavius flicked his eyes up at the hat. "It has a sweat stain right along the rim."

"Will do, sir."

"Good man."

Octavius got his coffee and headed for the executive suite, which was in the back of the large facility, down a long warehouse-like corridor with dull canned lights shining from high above. A splash of coffee burned his hand as he walked and he cursed. His large hands were trembling. He attributed it to nerves. He was uptight about the urgency in Mayor Marsden Maddox's voice when he'd called Octavius to set up the secretive meeting he was about to walk into. He'd blocked it out until now.

Although Octavius was in the business three ways with Mars and Timmy Kondore, he couldn't stand Timmy. As far as Octavius was concerned, Timmy was a disrespectful, spoiled, rich twerp living off of his parents' wealth. But Octavius knew a good deal when he saw one. When he and Mars had been looking for a third financial backer in their opioid business, Mars had arranged for Octavius to rent a yacht in St. Augustine and drive it up to Timmy in Charleston to give him a sample of their opioids. Little did Suzanne know when she sailed with him that the yacht was packed to the gills with hundreds of thousands of opioid pills that Octavius and Mars had received from a new source in China. If Timmy liked the goods, and if his distributors and clients liked the product, he would buy in as a third partner.

And that's exactly what happened.

For the past year, the three men had brought down more money than any of them knew what to do with. Their main product of choice, which delivered the biggest high to clients and the greatest return on their investment, was fentanyl. Mars had found a source in China that produced the fentanyl—along with hydrocodone, morphine, codeine, heroin, black heroin, and oxycodone—in its labs without government oversight. They then shipped it to a port in Mazatlán, Mexico, where it was put on trucks and transported to DoughWorx. Upstairs the drugs were tested, sorted, packaged, and prepped for distribution by truck to any of a dozen regional sellers. The best news of all the past year had been that Timmy had found various ways to sell the drugs directly to users via the internet and Dark Web, cutting out the middleman distributor completely and putting more profit in their pockets. So, they had a small division upstairs that had become known to the three of them as the 'online goldmine.'

Octavius got to the executive suite, stopped, closed his eyes with a fist on the door handle, took in an enormous breath, and exhaled long and slowly.

Clear your mind of everything . . .

He repeated the breathing exercise.

Positive thoughts . . .

He took another deep breath and plunged into the office.

"Good morning, gentlemen!" he said.

The huge floor to ceiling window allowed the crisp morning light to cast black shadows into the large, stately room—the focal point of which was a long, shiny executive table with twelve swivel chairs. Two coffee cups and plates with crumbs sat on the table.

"Octavius," Mars said.

"Big O," Timmy said.

Octavius hated that nickname.

Both men stood about fifteen feet apart and had their phones out.

"Shall we sit?" Octavius set his coffee down, pulled out a chair and did so.

At a slow clip, Mars and Timmy made their way to their chairs.

"Timmy, I'd appreciate it if you don't vape in here anymore," Octavius said. "It smells like a circus."

"It's funnel cake." Timmy sneered. "Whatever you say, Big O."

"Let's get right to it, gentlemen. We've got a problem," said Mars, who wore a navy suit, stark white shirt, leather suspenders, and pink tie. Mars was about five-feet, nine-inches and two hundred pounds. He was a wide, solid little fireplug with weathered skin from lots of golf and his own tanning bed. He had white ovals around his eyes from wearing sunglasses all the time and Octavius wondered if he realized how dreadful it looked.

Timmy simply watched nonchalantly, rocking back and forth, playing with a stretchy purple bracelet he'd taken off his wrist. He was a whisp of a kid, probably only late twenties. He had short, burnt orange hair, skin as white as an opioid pill, and pointy features—from his nose and chin to his elbows and knees. Also, one of his two blue eyes pointed a hair in the opposite direction of the other eye. Octavius always wondered if it might be glass but had no intention of asking the kid.

"What's wrong?" Octavius said. "You sounded . . . out of character on the phone."

Mars leaned over the table closer to the two men. "A seventeen-year-old girl died after taking some of our stuff," Mars said softly, seriously.

Both Octavius and Timmy sat up to attention and began asking questions.

Mars held up a hand, flashing a big silver Rolex. "Shh. Let me tell you what I know, then we'll talk." He cleared his throat, licked his fat lips, and swallowed hard. "As far as I've been able to narrow it down, it was a batch of China White she bought directly from the online goldmine."

"I told you it was a bad idea to get into that crap!" Octavius's face exploded with heat as he glared at Timmy. It was one thing to sell fentanyl and heroin separately, but Timmy had insisted they find a way to mix the two to create the popular China White, which brought a premium price.

"Will you shut up, please, until I finish?" Mars said.

Timmy just looked down at his heavy metal vape pipe that was now on the table, shook his head, smirked, and spun it repeatedly like a four-year-old.

"Six other orders of that batch went out, all bought online, and we've had no other reports of problems," Mars said. "That's the good news—that, hopefully, it was nothing in the product that killed her."

"She probably mixed it with alcohol or took too much," Timmy said.

Mars sighed and again held up a hand to quiet the others. "The bad news is, this girl's parents are coming after us with a vengeance."

Octavius felt sweat break out on his forehead as he envisioned the grieving, outraged father on the warpath. He wondered if somehow he might have given Suzanne some of the China White, which would explain why she'd been so out of it the night before.

"But they can't get to us," Timmy insisted. "There's no way they can trace us."

The three men had invested a ton of money to make their online sales "untraceable," thanks to the help of their computer guru friend, Lincoln.

"This girl's parents are very wealthy," Mars continued. "The father's a big-time Vegas attorney, an ambulance chaser who has many, many connections. Although we have a solid firewall, he's obviously paid big bucks to drill down deep enough to find out that the bad batch came from Arizona. This is the word on the street."

"He won't get any closer," Timmy said, looking down at his spinning pipe. He had Costa sunglasses on top of his head and wore skinny jeans, black leather high-tops, and a camel-colored suede coat with white fleece inside.

"From what I'm told," Mars said quietly, "this guy is devoting everything he has—all his money and clout—to find the distributor."

There was a knock at the door. It opened and Tate leaned in with his tall, dirty white hat. "Can I get you gentlemen anything?"

Timmy reached for his empty coffee cup and started to hold it up.

"No, Tate, thanks," Octavius waved him away. "We're good."

Tate left and closed the door.

"Timmy, this is your fault. You got greedy. You had to have China White," Octavius said. "We were fine without it—"

"I didn't hear you complaining when the money from it was rolling in, Big O," Timmy said.

"Stop arguing," Mars yelled in a low voice. "For now we need to stop producing China White and shut down the online goldmine, and I mean scrap it, destroy it—so there's no trace of it. We can bring it back later once we get through this. Timmy, can you arrange that?"

Timmy closed his eyes, pursed his lips, and shook his head. "I don't think that's necessary."

Octavius started to object, but Mars beat him to it. "Timmy, I'm not asking you. I'm telling you to shut it down."

Timmy shrugged. Without making eye contact he said, "I'll contact Lincoln."

"Good. Other sales to our distributors continue as usual," Mars said. "We'll assume the China White was clean and the girl made mistakes, overdosed. I'm keeping an eye on the girls' parents and how close they get; I'll keep you posted . . . Now, we have one more matter to discuss."

Timmy looked at his phone. "How long will this take?"

Mars shook his head and his mouth sealed shut. He heaved a sigh. His brown eyes leveled on Octavius. "We need to talk about Suzanne," Mars said. "She's talking too much."

17

JOANIE ENDED the call with daughter Leena and wandered to the front window of the Airbnb. Leena had said she and her brother Brandon were "okay but getting somewhat sick and tired of each other." Joanie smiled. Oldest son J.P. and his girlfriend Tammy were expected at their house in Portland that evening to spend the night with Brandon and Leena. They were all going to eat pizza and wings, drink soda, and binge Netflix.

Wayne glided around in the parking lot on the repaired bike to make sure the brakes were fixed. She knocked on the window. He wobbled and they waved to each other. He gave a thumbs up and pointed toward Red Rock City, where he told her he was going to take a ride and poke around. Thank God he hadn't complained about wearing the helmet that came with the rental bikes.

She watched him roll out onto the bike path, and quietly gave thanks—for their marriage, their kids, their home in Portland, and for all the many things with which they'd been blessed. She wanted Wayne to be done with police work. She didn't want him to take any more chances. The past three years had been the most dangerous she could remember—from the mass shooting at Pioneer Square to Leena's kidnapping, not to mention the recent run in with domestic violence maniac Blaine Milligan (now deceased).

To Joanie it was clear that now was the time to hang it up. They were both in good health and if Wayne took his pension now, one year shy of being fully vested, it would still be plenty of money, especially factoring in their savings and upcoming social security. She was quietly hoping he would see it that way, but so far on the trip he'd been unusually quiet about the topic. She'd tried to broach it several times, but he'd politely said he didn't want to talk about it; and the last thing she wanted to do was force her opinion on him. She wanted it to be his decision, so he wouldn't have any regrets. For now it felt like he was just so glad to be away from the job, and from Portland, that all he wanted to do was clear his head of police work and all the pressure that came with it.

Joanie microwaved the cup of tea she'd made earlier, unplugged the laptop, found the napkin she'd written on, and got situated at the table on the small, shaded back patio. She immediately noticed cigarette smoke drifting over from the tiny house next door. Even though it was warming up some as noon approached, it was still cool. She gave a fake cough and went back inside, threw a jacket on, and returned to her spot. She opened the laptop and began searching the name she'd scribbled on the napkin, Kondore.

After trying a variety of spellings, up popped an assortment of links about a young, ashen white man named Timothy Kondore of Charleston, South Carolina. She searched around until she found a feature story about him in a Sunday edition of Charleston's *Post and Courier*.

Timothy Kondore:
King of Charleston Harbor

He's young, he's wealthy, he's brash, and he loves fine food, fancy cars and fast boats. His name is Timothy Kondore, but he insists you call him "Timmy." Maybe that's because the 29-year-old millionaire is just a kid at heart.

Timmy's vast mansion, nestled on Sullivan's Island along the port of Charleston, is filled with "toys" from the Teslas and Maseratis in his seven-car garage, to the huge sauna, tennis court, pool and hot tub out back, to the many jet skis and watercrafts along the coastline. But those are nothing compared to the "baby" he has parked at Serenity Bay Boat

Yard in Charleston, where he keeps his seventy-foot, tri-deck luxury yacht, complete with enormous sky lounge.

The name Kondore is familiar to many Carolinians due to the wealth and notoriety of Timmy's father, Dallas P. Kondore III, who's amassed a fortune in commercial real estate throughout the southeast. Timmy graduated from the prestigious Harbor Town Academy in 2010 and attended the University of North Carolina in Wilmington, but dropped out after one year.

"College wasn't for me," Timmy said while sipping an espresso and periodically tweaking a purple wristband at one of Charleston's most posh outdoor cafes. "I was ready to get started with my life. Why wait another three years when I could be out there making money, building an empire?"

He worked for the family real estate business for several years while, on the side, getting his own luxury boat business off the ground (Kondore Luxury Lines Limited in Charleston). Since then he's become a diverse entrepreneur, venturing into all kinds of startup businesses—from an online dating app (SyncUp), to a computer software development firm (DataDrive), to an artisan bread company (DoughWorx) in Sedona, Arizona.

Timmy works hard and plays hard. He loves deep sea fishing, scuba diving, grand prix racing, sailing, jet skiing, and tennis. As much as he's outside, you'd think his skin would be as leathery brown as that of his good friend—Jessup Mayor Marsden Maddox, but instead, he is shockingly fair. "I was born with a severe sun allergy," he said. "I have to wear long sleeve shirts, hats, wet suit pants, and prescription suntan lotion. If I go out without those things, I can have a fatal reaction."

Tragically, when Timmy was 10 he lost his left eye in a fishing accident while on a deep sea excursion with his parents. He jokes about the incident now, as he points to the artificial blue eye that replaced the one he lost as a boy.

Joanie skimmed the rest of the article and made sure there was nothing more about Octavius. There were all kinds of articles on Timmy and the Kondore real estate empire.

Buried in an article in a bi-weekly online newspaper from Folly Beach, South Carolina, Joanie learned Timmy had been arrested in a drug bust near the Folly Beach pier in 2017. He was caught selling a "large quantity" of prescription painkillers from one of his boats to undercover cops. Joanie followed the story thread over the next seven months and learned Timmy's father's legal dream team got Timmy off with a slap on the wrist and six months of community service, during which time he'd been required to wear a GPS-monitored ankle bracelet.

Joanie leaned back and sighed. She sipped her tea and stared at the immense Red Rock Mountains. The cigarette smoker next door must've gone inside. *So, this rich kid Timmy Kondore is in business with Octavius and Jessup Mayor Marsden Maddox . . . And he's the one to whom Octavius and Suzanne delivered the yacht when they sailed it from St. Augustine to Charleston.*

Suzanne had said she and Octavius had become close friends with Mayor Maddox and his wife. Joanie searched Mayor Marsden Maddox. The first story she read provided a boring description of how the 52-year-old had been elected as mayor in the city of Jessup in 2020, following a long and successful career as a plastic surgeon.

Interestingly, Maddox had his own website at MarsdenMaddox.com. There was even an image gallery. It looked like his much younger wife, Candace, had obviously been taking advantage of her husband's plastic surgeon skills. She had dark hair with auburn streaks, an expensive cut, and her body appeared sculpted of stone. They looked to be a very charismatic couple, always dressed in fine clothes and looking flawless out on the town.

Joanie left the website thinking how vain it was for the mayor to have his own website, but then again, he was a politician and she guessed that's probably what they all did; she'd never thought about it before.

Okay. Joanie took in a deep breath, exhaled, and got focused on

Octavius Hunt. Since Suzanne had slipped and called him Freddie, that's where she started, searching every variation of the name spelling for Freddie Hunt. It was a common name. As she opened link after link and continued to strike out, she figured that if he changed his first name, he probably changed his last name, too.

She searched Octavius Hunt again and found exactly what she'd found last time—his life from two years ago until the present—nothing before. When she saw the mention of his artisan bread company, she searched the name of it, DoughWorx. She found a feature story about it in an online magazine about Sedona. It showed photos of the large, contemporary building from the outside, constructed of red brick matching the surrounding Sedona backdrop and lots of dark glass, with rocks, cactus, and local plants dotting the landscape.

The story mentioned the many different kinds of bread and specialty items the company baked on site, and how some items were distributed to stores and restaurants within a one-hundred-mile radius. It told about the spacious, lodge-like café that was almost always filled with locals and tourists. A fraction of the story gave mention to the three owners, but Joanie learned nothing new about them from the piece.

She stood and took her teacup inside. She added water to the kettle, put it on the burner, and turned it on. She checked her phone—no messages. She paced and thought as she waited for the water to boil.

She thought of Suzanne at the airport, heading to see her Uncle Steve back in Bend, Oregon, where they'd grown up together. She pictured Suzanne's mom Barbara, and her cozy house, which Joanie knew almost as well as her own.

The kettle began to creak, and the water started a low rumble. Joanie was ninety-eight percent sure Octavius wouldn't try to contact them again—not without Suzanne. They weren't his type. And they certainly didn't want to see him again. She recalled how he took her hand and led her up to that ridge to look at Venus. *Downright weird.*

He gave her the creeps.

She turned off the burner and poured hot water into her cup. Maybe it was time to drop the whole thing, like Wayne suggested.

Get on with vacation. She set the tea down and went to the patio to get the laptop. She thought perhaps she would ride her bike into town and try to find Wayne, maybe have lunch.

She grabbed the laptop and napkin from the patio and returned inside. In the bathroom, she freshened up her makeup and brushed her hair. She found her purse and put her driver's license and a credit card in the pocket of her jacket, then went to find her phone. When she did, it dawned on her that she still remembered Suzanne's home telephone number from when they were kids—before cell phones.

It would be nice to say hello to Suzanne's mom—and possibly even get her take on Suzanne's state of mind.

On a whim, Joanie decided to try the number.

It's probably changed by now.

This would be Joanie's good deed of the day. She could tell Barbara she's praying for Uncle Steve and give her a laugh by reminding her of those big pickle jars he'd brought to that family picnic.

Joanie dialed the number.

I'll tell her I saw Suzanne.

It was ringing!

18

Suzanne was gliding high, not a care in the world. Tate had refilled her coffee by the toasty fireplace in the DoughWorx café, and she'd been knee-deep in a suspense novel she was reading on her phone. At the end of a chapter cliffhanger near the middle of the book, she practically gasped aloud and put the phone down with a loud sigh, then laughed at herself for making such a commotion about a book.

She needed a break from the tension so she stood and walked over to the order area. "Tate, will my stuff be okay there? I need to stretch." She pointed to her leather bag on the couch.

"Absolutely, Miss Suzanne. I'll keep an eye on it," he said.

"Thank you." She wished he would drop the 'Miss.' It made her feel old.

She sipped her coffee and wandered to a large picture window. It was a cool but gorgeous day outside. She wondered what Joanie and Wayne would do the rest of the day? When she started to think about what she'd done at breakfast with Joanie, how she'd lied about having to leave town, she abruptly turned and examined the large café. She looked at all the different people and masterfully steered her mind away from her shame.

Smooth jazz played on the sound system and people throughout the café were in various forms of conversation—some deep and intense, others upbeat with laughter. The space was subtly decorated for the holidays with tiny white lights and wreaths here and there. Octavius knew his clientele would expect some acknowledgement of the season, but he hated Christmas—and anything to do with formal religion.

Late one night when he'd had way too much to drink at StoneSpell, he'd confided to her that he'd had an unforgettable and life-altering experience in the church when he was a boy. When his father left home for good, his mother began taking his sister and him to church. His mom found solace there, and Octavius gradually made new friends at the youth group and even served as an acolyte. He was fourteen at the time and the church helped fill the void left by his absent father. He said it had awakened such a joy in him and so changed his life that he considered going into ministry. That was, until he faced the sobering and repulsive advances of Father Pat, a graying but physically powerful priest who sexually abused him on at least four occasions.

Because of Octavius's devastating experience with the priest, Suzanne had not only understood, but gone along with his interest in meditation, self-exploration, and the healing powers emanating from the Red Rocks. She still believed in God, but because of Octavius, she'd opened her mind to believe that every person needed to find their own god or higher power—whatever that may be—in order to cope with life and all the difficulties it threw at them.

Suzanne knew pain killers had become her master, but she shook the truth away and walked into the dimly lit hallway where the restrooms were, turned the corner, and passed the sign that read, 'Employees Only.' She looked down the long, quiet warehouse-like corridor, figuring Octavius was in the executive suite at the far end of the hall.

She decided to use the restroom and get back to her book when a door suddenly swung open in the dark hallway; a door she didn't even realize existed. A stocky Hispanic man with a buzz cut and manicured beard came through the door wearing a white apron. He scowled, mumbled something in Spanish, and headed in the direction of the restrooms.

Suzanne caught the metal door just before it locked closed. She looked to see if the man had noticed, but he'd ducked into the restroom. The door and its handle were black, the same color as the walls. There was a small, electronic box to the left of the door and Suzanne guessed the only way in was with a remote key fob.

She stepped inside the fluorescent lit stairwell which revealed a staircase leading upward. She'd never realized there was occupied space on the second story of the building. Since she had time to kill and felt she had the freedom—after all, this was Octavius's business—she headed up the stairs to see what was up there and heard the door lock shut behind her.

As she got near the top of the steps, Suzanne heard the rumble of machinery. She wondered if more baking went on up there that she didn't know about, or if perhaps Octavius and his partners rented the space out to another company. She came to restrooms and saw bright daylight shining around the corner. An unpleasant odor wafted in the air. She walked toward the light and around the corner.

Enormous skylights lined the ceiling and ran the length of the football field-sized chamber. Suzanne stood dumbfounded. She counted three men working around the vast room, each wearing a white apron and hood, and a clear facemask. The concrete floor was dusted in a white powdery substance, which Suzanne assumed at first was flour.

But then reality began to sink in.

Silver tables lined both sides of the vast space and on the tables was a plethora of silver trays filled with blue, pink, white, and green pills, all shapes and sizes of glass containers and tubing, blenders, scales, thermometers, silver pots, white plastic funnels, cans, plastic bags, and huge blue plastic drums. Paper plates with different colors of ink spots on them were scattered all over the floor.

Suzanne stood there frozen, taking it all in—fighting against the reality of what she was seeing.

Through a thin white haze that hung in the air, conveyor belts of various sizes rumbled along throughout the room carrying pills of all colors. Her eyes fell to a long white machine where the pills went in mixed together, but came out the other end, bagged in clear plastic bags, each containing hundreds of pills of the same color, and stamped with white labels. Another silver machine with a huge bin at the top jerked and turned and vibrated and loudly stamped out foil packets of pills by the dozens.

"Hey!" a male voice shouted from behind.

The other two men heard and looked up.

All three glared at her shocked, as if she'd risen from the dead.

The Hispanic man who'd passed her to use the restroom was ten feet away and approaching fast, yelling in Spanish with his hands in the air like he was going to throttle her.

"No está permitido aquí!" he spit as he yelled so loudly that the veins at the base of his neck protruded. He yelled something more in Spanish.

She threw her hands up in defense and heard various pieces of machinery groan to a halt around the large room. She turned back and one of the men was yelling into his phone in Spanish, pointing at Suzanne. The other man across the room yelled, "Fuera! Fuera!" and rushed toward her.

Suzanne's right arm was squeezed hard and the man who'd gone to the restroom spun her around and jerked her toward the steps. "No está permitido aquí!" he yelled. "Estás en problemas!"

"It's okay, it's okay!" Suzanne yelled. "I'm leaving. I'm leaving." She shook her arm free and pointed in his face. "Leave me alone, okay? I'm going. I'm Octavius's girlfriend."

The man pointed right back at her, yelling in Spanish, pointing downstairs.

Suzanne took one last look at the enormous operation. All three of the other men were now hurrying toward her.

She hit the steps running.

SITTING in the executive suite having learned of the girl's overdose and death—and that her attorney father was in hot pursuit of the seller—Octavius was already frustrated. Then Mars mentioned Suzanne had been talking too much. Octavius shot to his feet. "What do you mean she's talking too much? Where do you get this?"

Mars glanced at a grinning Timmy, who was leaning back lazily in his chair with his eyes fixed on the spinning pipe on the table.

Mars leveled his eyes on Octavius. "Candace has heard Suzanne, on more than one occasion, telling other women about how you provide her with oxy."

As far as Octavius was concerned, Mars's wife Candace was as phony as a three-dollar bill and existed only to spend money and gossip. Plastic surgery had become such an obsession with her that she looked like a mannequin. She was half Mars's age and had long been playing him as her Sugar Daddy.

"Is that so?" Octavius said. "And who *exactly* did Candace hear Suzanne telling this to?"

"Women at the Standard Club," Mars said.

The Standard Club was a private golf, tennis, dining, and social club. Octavius had joined at Suzanne's urging, because she wanted to take tennis lessons. They dined there perhaps once a month and Suzanne sometimes went there to work-out or enjoy a cocktail (or four) by the pool now and then. Octavius never much cared for it because the members were mostly businesspeople, none of whom had a creative bone in their falsely sculpted bodies.

"And what was Suzanne reported to have said, exactly, and to whom?" Octavius said.

"Let's not get into the weeds. The bottom line is Suzanne's raising eyebrows about you getting your hands on oxy—and that endangers all of us and this operation," Mars said with authority. "We can't have it and we want to know what you're going to do about it?"

"Yeah," Timmy chimed in with a smirk, snatching up the pipe. "What're you gonna do about it, Big O?"

Mars's phone vibrated.

Octavius said, "I find it difficult to believe Suzanne would say anything to anyone about—"

"Octavius stop!" Mars demanded, reaching for the buzzing phone. "You've let Suzanne's usage get *way* out of control. Candace has seen her, frankly, in *pitiful* condition. She's not looking good. She *looks* like an addict. It can't go on. She's jeopardizing the whole operation."

The statement hit Octavius as if he'd been splashed with a bucket of ice water.

"Loose lips sink ships," Timmy added.

In that instant, Octavius realized they were probably right. Suzanne didn't look healthy. She was full-on addicted to pain killers and, after one too many drinks, he could picture her blabbing to the other women. He'd always believed she talked too much.

Mars glanced at his phone, scowled, and sat up in his chair.

Octavius pondered what exactly Mars meant when he demanded to know what Octavius was going to do about Suzanne.

"Look," Octavius declared, "I will talk to her about this—today. I guarantee it won't happen again." He was ticked now and already scheming about the various ways he would reprimand Suzanne.

"Hola?" Mars answered his phone, which he never did during meetings, so it must've been one of the guys upstairs. "Qué?" Mars yelled. He jumped to his feet, tipping his chair over. "Keep her there!" he yelled into his phone. "Manténgala allí!"

A chill ran down Octavius's spine and his forehead broke out in sweat.

Mars clenched his teeth and he sneered at Octavius. "Suzanne's been upstairs!"

19

Joanie stood motionless and oddly a bit anxious in the kitchen of the Sedona tiny house waiting to see if anyone would pick up the phone at Suzanne's childhood home in Bend, Oregon.

After several more rings, an elderly woman said hello and Joanie knew instantly it was Suzanne's mom from the sound of her familiar voice.

"Hello, is this Barbara?" Joanie said gaily.

"It is, who's calling?"

"Mrs. Bartholomew, hi! This is Joanie . . . Carter, your old neighbor."

"Oh, dear goodness, Joanie. How good to hear your voice. What a pleasant surprise."

"I can't believe you have the same number," Joanie said. "I actually just called on a whim. My name's not Carter anymore, it's Deetz."

"I know, I know. Suzanne's kept me up to date, somewhat. Well, she used to, anyway. You're in Portland, aren't you? I saw your husband on the news after that tragic shooting several years ago."

"We are, but we're actually in Sedona on vacation right now."

"Oh, wonderful. So, you'll get to see Suzanne—if you can pry her away from that artist boyfriend."

Joanie thought it was odd Barbara gave no hint she was the least bit down about her brother Steve's critical condition, or that Suzanne was on her way home.

"I had breakfast with her today, before she left for the airport," Joanie said.

"Oh, fantastic," Barbara said. "Where is she headed?"

Words escaped Joanie.

Maybe Barbara has Alzheimer's? But she seems so sharp . . .

"Home. To Bend."

"What?"

"She said Uncle Steve . . . isn't well," Joanie said.

"Steve? My brother? From what? What happened?" Barbara said, alarmed.

Joanie felt awful. She quickly explained. "Suzanne said Uncle Steve had a heart attack yesterday and he's in serious condition. Her boyfriend Octavius was taking her to the airport this morning so she could fly home to see him. I assumed you knew all this, I'm so, so sorry."

"She didn't tell me she was coming. I better call Steve. Why would I not know about this? Surely Nikki would've called me. I better run, Joanie."

Joanie started to apologize again, but the line went dead.

She stared at her phone.

Suzanne lied to me?

Nikki was Steve's wife and, yes, she certainly would have let Barbara know by now if he was in the hospital.

Joanie wanted to tell Wayne everything, but not over the phone.

She thought about calling Suzanne, but she was so mad. And, why bother? If Suzanne was going to lie and dodge her—forget it!

The entire situation was bizarre.

Octavius was bizarre.

Suzanne had changed so much.

People *do* change, Joanie told herself. But Suzanne didn't *look* well. She was pale and scratching. She was aloof. She didn't have the light in her eyes that she'd always had. She didn't *sound* like herself.

It was almost as if the Holy Spirit had left her—or was being squelched.

Joanie's stomach growled. She checked the time and decided to blow off the bike ride and make lunch while she thought things through. She got salad fixings out of the fridge and texted Wayne to ask if he wanted her to make him a salad. While she waited for his response, she got two plates down and began making her own. But she couldn't get her mind off the fact that Barbara didn't know Steve had had a heart attack and didn't know Suzanne was on her way to Bend.

Joanie's phone rang. It was Wayne. He said he was on his way and would love a "Joanie salad."

"You are not going to believe the latest on Suzanne," Joanie said.

"Okay. I'm off to the side of the bike path. I'll be back in ten minutes. Tell me over lunch, okay?"

Wayne was being so patient with her.

The second they hung up, Joanie's phone rang again. The screen showed it was Suzanne's mother calling.

"Hey, Barbara," Joanie answered.

"Joanie, I wanted to get right back to you. I just spoke to Steve and he's fine."

Joanie reeled.

"No heart attack. No hospital. And neither of us know anything about Suzanne coming home. Are you sure she said it was her Uncle Steve, my brother, not someone else? A friend perhaps?"

Joanie closed her eyes and a hand went to her forehead. She was so angry at Suzanne, who'd obviously lied. And she was embarrassed for having gotten fragile Barbara all worked up.

"I'm so sorry, Barbara. Yes, she said it was Uncle Steve. We confirmed he was the one, we even talked about the big pickle jars he brought to a picnic at your house one time. I hate to say this, but maybe Suzanne just made it up because she didn't want to see me any more—while we're out here."

"You don't think she's coming home?" Barbara said.

"No, I don't. Again, I'm sorry to have gotten your hopes up, and to scare you about the other thing."

"Joanie, have you met her boyfriend?"

"Wayne and I had dinner at his house. Suzanne's car broke down so she didn't make it."

Silence.

"Barbara?"

Silence.

"Barbara, are you there?"

"I'm . . . The exact same thing happened when we were out there," Barbara said. "Dennis and I were supposed to have dinner with them at Octavius's house and Suzanne cancelled at the last minute. He told us her car broke down. She never came."

Joanie's mind dissolved to white and she felt hot.

"When were you here, Barbara?" she finally said. "How did Suzanne seem to you?"

"Summer. July. So hot. She was not well." Barbara broke down. "She was not good."

Joanie had *known* something was wrong!

"I'm sorry," Barbara blurted. "She was just . . . I think they must take drugs, smoke marijuana, something . . ." She cried.

"It's okay, Barbara. Suzanne hasn't seemed like herself to me, either. Not at all."

"Really? So it wasn't just me?" Barbara sniffed, took in a deep breath, and sighed.

"No," Joanie said. "I don't know what it is, but she's . . . not herself."

"She's hiding something," Barbara said. "And what about him? He's basically convinced her not to go to church anymore. She had a great church when she first got out there, before she met him. He gave me the worst feeling, as if his whole life's just an act. Where does he get all his money? Selling paintings? There's no way."

Joanie was tracking right along with her.

"Dennis tried to dig deeper with him about his work, his income, his background—and he got nowhere," Barbara said.

"We're striking out, too."

"Really? My goodness that makes me feel better. Confirmation. I've been thinking I'm going crazy."

"I don't think so." Joanie pictured Suzanne staggering into her apartment complex with Octavius. Would Barbara and Dennis be furious if they knew stuff like that was going on.

Joanie heard the key in the lock, and Wayne yelled, "Hello." He rounded the corner wheeling his bike right into the kitchen. Joanie threw up a hand as if to ask what he was thinking of, and pointed that she was on the phone.

"You said she doesn't seem like herself," Barbara said. "What's been wrong when you've seen her? What's she been like?"

"I'm not sure. I've only seen her twice. Once was for ten minutes when we first got here and then we had breakfast today. The first time she was just kind of . . . detached, distant. I mean, she was happy, very happy, but just not at all like herself. Not at all interested in me or Wayne. You know her, she always asks how you're doing and she's such a great listener."

Barbara chimed in. "We met them for dinner one night while we were there and you would have thought she'd been drinking all day. She was slurring her words and practically falling asleep. My husband was so upset. Octavius just kept trying to charm us and leave her out of the conversation. It was so upsetting. I've been worried sick."

"Well, I wish I could have seen her more, but it doesn't look like it was meant to be," Joanie said.

"This Octavius . . . something is very off about him," Barbara said. "I could feel it within minutes of meeting him. I got the worst headache when we met. It was as if God was giving me a warning. I'm going to call her when we hang up. She told you she was flying to Bend, I'm going to call her bluff. Really. I've got to get to the bottom of this. If she needs help, I need to get her help."

Wayne had picked up where Joanie left off and was fixing their salads.

"Well, if you find out anything, if you reach her, let me know," Joanie said. "She's pretty much been ignoring my calls and texts. I really want to know what's going on. Please, don't hesitate to ring me."

They ended the call and Joanie leaned over on the counter where Wayne was finishing the salads.

"That was Suzanne's mom."

Wayne dropped his head back and closed his eyes. "No, you didn't."

"Wayne, Uncle Steve didn't have a heart attack. And I don't think Suzanne's on her way to Bend. I think she's right here in Sedona."

20

Suzanne busted through the door at the bottom of the steps inside DoughWorx, stumbled, got her bearings, and ran back toward the café, her mind blown by the major drug operation she'd just walked into upstairs.

At the restrooms she glanced back, her heart thundering. The men from upstairs were not following—yet. One had been calling someone on his phone.

She hurried back to the café, slowing to a walk but still breathing hard when she came in view of the many patrons. Tate watched her from behind the counter. Her face was red-hot and he could probably tell she was flustered. She gave a nervous smile, moved quickly back to the couch, got her leather bag, and headed for the sliding glass doors at a steady clip—not caring if Tate was still watching.

The cold air hit her. She wanted it to sober her.

If she had keys to Octavius's car, she would have taken it to get out of there. She fumbled for her phone and, with trembling hands, clicked open the Uber app and requested the first available ride back to her apartment; she would figure out what to do from there.

She spun around to see if she was being pursued but saw no one coming from inside. She needed to get away from that building. She was so distraught she started walking, the length of the building, then into the parking lot and toward the road.

Get away.

The sun was bright. It felt good mixed with the cold. She was taking short, choppy breaths and told herself to breathe deeply.

This is your wakeup call.

Suzanne knew deep within that she was addicted to the pain killers, but she hadn't been ready to face it. Why should she? Octavius had given her everything—from her apartment to her wardrobe, fine food, nice things, and all her bills paid with no questions asked. She'd been floating along carefree as if on a cloud watching the world go by.

Watching yourself self-destruct.

She looked back as she walked faster and faster.

No one yet.

She put on her sunglasses. Her hands shook ridiculously as she typed a note to the Uber driver telling him that she'd started to walk west along the paved bike path. Her phone showed a map with the driver just four minutes out.

She'd become Octavius's puppet, or had she? He thought she didn't realize he was using her. But she knew. And she had also known that nothing long-term would likely come of their relationship. In her distorted view, she'd been the one using him!

In the recesses of her warped mind, she'd always understood she couldn't go on like this. The pills were taking their toll on her—physically, mentally, and spiritually. She'd done nothing productive with her life for more than a year and was only living for the next hit of oxy.

Worst of all, she'd fallen away from God. Right along with Octavius, she'd been worshipping herself and the earth rather than the one who'd created it all. As if to exaggerate the point, at that exact moment a semitruck blew past her, the wind from it nearly knocking her off her feet. Still wavering from the blast of wind and the smell of gas, she looked at her phone—the Uber driver was two minutes out. His name was Malik and he would be driving a black Prius.

She debated what to do when she got home. One option was to pack a bag and go to the rehab clinic she'd researched online several weeks ago. She'd found one in Sedona with high ratings and reviews, but it was extremely expensive. Since she had no savings, she had previously contemplated approaching Octavius to see if he would fund her stay, but she knew deep down that he did not want her straight, otherwise he would have helped her get clean by now. She certainly couldn't ask him for help now, so that wasn't an option. She needed to get away from there. Her best bet would probably be to go home to Bend and seek help there, near her Mom and family.

She hated herself for lying to Joanie that morning and it dawned on her how sick she must be to have done so to one of her very best friends, just so she could continue to cover up her addiction. She could call Joanie and ask for help, but the last thing Joanie and Wayne needed on their vacation was to babysit a drug addict who belonged in rehab.

Suzanne was starting to feel the need for a bump. That was the thing about oxy, she always knew the *instant* it was wearing off. And with her, that time seemed to diminish between each hit. Every day she realized she was building up a tolerance to it, because she needed more of it, more frequently.

Coming down from the high was the exact opposite of being high. Everything hurt, physically, mentally, and emotionally. Small problems seemed monstrous. She stressed frantically about *everything*—until she got that next hit. Then, magically, once she did, nothing mattered, or bothered her, or hurt.

How would she stay off it without help, without professionals to guide her through the detox phase? She'd read that users should not attempt to quit cold turkey, that intervention was needed, including supervised detox and therapy.

The night in Octavius's basement came flooding back to her.

Those women . . .

She'd put them out of her mind a million times since then, but they were *real*. They were there!

Who were they?

His prisoners?

Could she end up down there?

By running out of DoughWorx, Suzanne had crossed a line. If or when Octavius caught up with her, he would know she'd discovered the drug operation.

She spotted a black car coming toward her in the distance and looked at the map showing the location of Malik's vehicle on her phone.

It's him. Thank God.

As the black Prius approached, sporting a Christmas wreath attached to the front grill, Suzanne waved both arms as if trying to flag down a helicopter in a forest fire.

The car slowed on the opposite side of the road and the driver's window went down. "Suzanne?" called the dark-skinned driver. He wore sunglasses and a Santa hat. He had a thick black beard and was hunched over as if he probably stood six-feet, six-inches tall.

"Yes! Malik?" She started to look both ways to cross the road.

"No, don't come over. Hold on. I'll turn around and get you."

"No, wait!"

But he sped off.

Suzanne turned to watch him go and a dark gray sedan caught her eye in the distance. It was barreling toward her like a pulsing stock car on its last-ditch approach to the checkered flag, engulfed in gas fumes that made it look like a mirage on the mountainous horizon.

Malik made a U-turn but must not have realized how fast the gray car was coming. Fear pulsed in Suzanne's temples as she watched the approaching gray vehicle swerve around Malik's Prius, roar past, then weave and lock back into its lane like a slot car on steroids.

Alarms roared in Suzanne's head.

It's them!

She heard the car's engine thundering toward her and almost threw up. She swallowed the bile and coughed violently. The base of her throat burned, and her eyes watered as she searched frantically for somewhere to hide—but there was nothing but rocky ground as far as she could see. She could only stand there out in the open, hoping the dark car would fly past her like the truck had.

When the car was one hundred yards away its flashers went on and Suzanne heard its engine let up.

It's slowing down!

It pulled off to the side of the highway and slowly headed straight for her.

The Prius driven by Malik was not far behind.

Suzanne stood there, helpless.

The shiny gray Audi S8 rolled to a stop. Through the front windshield Suzanne made out Mayor Marsden Maddox at the wheel and Timmy Kondore in the passenger seat. The side windows were black.

The back door opened and Octavius unfolded from the car, held his hands up, and began walking toward her slowly, as if approaching a dangerous dog. "What's going on, baby?"

Suzanne put on her happy act, pointed and nodded toward the black Prius, which had pulled up and stopped behind the mayor's Audi. "Your meeting was taking forever." Her voice sounded hideously high and she knew she was a frantic mess. She cleared her throat. "I called an Uber, it's here now."

Octavius hadn't heard the Prius pull up and turned to look.

That's when Suzanne gathered her courage and started walking toward it.

Octavius turned back around and put his hands up to stop her right when she got to him. "Hold on. Hold on. We're good now. Everything's okay." Octavius turned and waved for the Uber driver to leave, then looked back at Suzanne. "You can come with us now. They'll take us back to my car and we'll get on with our day. Okay? Sound like a plan?"

She glanced through the windshield of the Audi and noticed Timmy and Mars swiveled around looking back at the Prius.

"I'm not feeling great," Suzanne put a hand to her stomach. "Let me have this guy take me back to my place." She continued toward the Prius. "I just want to rest a bit. We can catch up later."

Octavius squeezed her right arm. "It's about time for another bump, isn't it?" He was trying to smile but spoke through clenched teeth. "Come on. I've got some of that good China White I told you about."

"Stop. That hurts!" Suzanne snapped her arm away.

"Hey, excuse me!" Malik had gotten out and was standing between his open door and the Prius. "Are you coming, Suzanne?"

"No, she's not," Octavius yelled. "Sorry about that, she has a ride. You can go." Octavius waved impatiently for Malik to leave again. "Go on! Charge us if you want."

"I want to go with him." Suzanne began walking toward Malik again.

"Suzanne, stop!" Octavius grabbed her wrist and wrenched it till it burned.

"Stop!" She tried to pull away, but he was too strong.

All in one swift motion, Timmy's door bounced open, and he headed toward them. "Get in here, now! We're leaving."

Suzanne looked at Timmy's pointy pale face in shock and felt her face burn with terror.

Timmy got within a foot of Suzanne. "Get in the car, *now*." He looked at Malik and yelled, "Go on, Santa. We don't need you. Scram!"

Malik gently closed his door and took several steps toward Suzanne. "It looks like she wants to come with me," he called.

"I do!" Suzanne yelled, hoping Malik might come help her.

Malik began walking toward them. He was indeed well over six feet tall and at least two-hundred pounds. Considering the seriousness of the situation, his drooping Santa hat was almost comical.

"Suzanne, don't do this," Octavius seethed, squeezed her wrist, and began pulling her. "Get in the car!"

Suzanne braced her legs and pulled with all her weight in the opposite direction.

"Hey man, leave her alone!" Malik was within twenty yards. "She's coming with me."

"Get back in your car!" Timmy yelled at Malik.

"Calm down, man." Malik held his hands out chest-high but continued approaching. "Let the lady go."

In a flash, Timmy reached into his coat, yanked out a black gun, and blasted it right over Malik's head.

The shot echoed in Suzanne's chest and Octavius cowered, his hands to his ears.

Malik dropped to the ground, his hat fell off, and he scrambled to his car without it.

Timmy fired again.

Suzanne screamed.

The bullet exploded the pavement twelve feet to the right of Malik, who'd made it into the Prius.

Suzanne broke into tears.

"Enough!" Octavius barked.

Timmy and Octavius each grabbed an arm and wrestled Suzanne toward the car.

Malik ducked and covered his head with one arm as his car whirred backward.

Suzanne's only hope was driving away.

21

Lunch always tasted better on vacation. Deetz and Joanie had enjoyed their salads on the back porch, he'd had a twenty-minute nap, and they were hiking Sedona's Roundabout Trail in the bright afternoon Arizona sunshine. They each wore sunglasses and light backpacks, which Joanie had filled with water bottles, fruit, and granola bars. Deetz wore shorts, Joanie had on leggings, and they both wore jackets.

Since Deetz's sense of direction was terrible, he stopped periodically to look back at the way they'd come so he would remember the way back to the public parking lot where they'd parked. There were many junctions on the trail where hikers could branch off to follow various trails. The two-mile loop they chose was considered an "easy" hike, during which they'd seen pinyon pines, junipers, and boulder fields.

"Wayne, come here," Joanie said, standing on the edge of the mesa overlooking Dry Creek. "See over there," she pointed, "that's Doe Mountain and that's Bear Mountain." She took pictures with her phone.

Deetz took in the surreal landscape and the brilliant blue sky. It was a good time of year to come, not too hot yet. The mountains were vast, large clusters of red sandstone, and the distinct layers amazed him and made him think of the flood recorded in Genesis when the whole earth was covered in water; even the very highest point had been twenty to forty feet under water.

Deetz took a deep breath. It did him so much good to get away from home, out of the routine, away from police work. Several other hikers stopped to admire the view of the cliffs and canyons, and the dry, prickly, green foliage that carpeted the view.

Joanie was so pretty and vibrant. She'd struck up a conversation with another hiker and had offered to take photos with the woman's phone, of she and her husband and sons with the mountains in the background.

Although Deetz was just one year away from retiring from the Portland Police Department and receiving the generous pension he'd worked toward for thirty-five years, Joanie wanted him to quit and take a reduced package. They'd not talked about it much on the trip, but he knew how she felt. The past three years had been extremely traumatic—and dangerous.

The problem was Deetz wasn't certain he was ready to hang it up. He'd always loved his work. He was the kind of person who needed to stay busy. He was afraid he would be bored to death if he retired now. Plus, he didn't like leaving things unfinished.

As he soaked in the scenery and sunlight, he admitted he was feeling his age, which he'd never thought much about before. He had dental work that needed to be done. His skin doctor had prescribed lotion to address pre-cancerous spots on his head. His knees were starting to hurt on his morning runs. He had borderline high blood pressure. He'd gained five pounds, which he blamed on his slowing metabolism. His mounting ailments were almost comical.

Joanie said goodbye to the family, came over, and put her arms around him.

"Isn't it beautiful?" she said.

"It is. You meet new friends everywhere you go, don't you?"

She chuckled and kissed him.

"Are you having fun?"

"It feels really good to be out here. I wouldn't want to live here, but it's beautiful to see."

"You're about to get really mad at me." She looked up at him and gave a nervous smile.

"Uh-oh. Why?"

"I can't stop thinking about Suzanne. I just can't."

Wayne tried to hide his frustration.

"I think she might have been on drugs that first time we saw her, and maybe even today at breakfast. Her mom even thinks she may be using."

Deetz sighed and his shoulders slumped. He wanted to be done with the whole Suzanne saga.

"Something she said is bugging me," Joanie said. "When she and Octavius took that boat to that Timmy guy in Charleston they got into a storm, huge waves. She wanted to call the Coast Guard and he refused. Why?"

Deetz shrugged and threw up his hands. "Because he's a guy and he just wanted to plow through it."

"What if he had drugs on the boat? What if he's a dealer?"

"Come on, honey. You're thinking too much about this."

"That would explain all his money. You can't tell me he's made millions on artwork. No way, not a chance. And why can't we find anything about him online from before Sedona?"

"Let's back up. You planned to see Suzanne. You came out here. Here we are. We went to the dinner, which she didn't show up for. You had breakfast. You've done all you can do. If she did lie about flying to Bend today, she obviously doesn't want to see you anymore. I'm sorry to say that. It's harsh, but it's reality. And besides, you don't know she didn't go. Maybe she's going to surprise her mom or something."

"Why wouldn't she just tell me that? She blatantly lied about her uncle being sick. Why would she do that?"

Deetz raised his eyebrows and shook his head.

"Something's going on," Joanie said.

Deetz shrugged. He was sick of talking about Suzanne and, frankly, was mad at her.

Joanie turned away and paced.

"What do you want to do, honey?" Deetz said. "You can't force your way into her life if she doesn't want you there."

"She's been one of my best friends since we were kids. If she's on drugs I need to help her."

"By doing what, though? If she is on drugs, she wants to be. Otherwise, she would have asked for your help."

"How many people addicted to drugs ask for help? That's what friends are for; they get involved in the messy stuff. They intervene."

"But, this is our vacation." And, the second Deetz said it, he felt like a spoiled brat.

She snapped back, "You don't have to do anything. My gosh."

Deetz felt like a selfish child.

Joanie didn't care if it was her vacation, she was concerned about the well-being, the life, of a friend.

"I'm sorry, babe," he said. "What do you think you want to do?"

"I know, I get it. It *is* your vacation—and I know how badly you need it. Maybe I'll just try calling her again. If I get her, I'm calling her out on the lie about going to Bend. And I may flat out ask her if she's doing drugs. What do I have to lose?"

Deetz nodded, silently hoping Joanie wouldn't reach Suzanne.

"I'll try her when we get back to the place," Joanie said.

Deetz did wonder about Octavius and all his money. He was probably in debt up to his ears.

"Come over here. Give me your phone," he said. "Let's get a picture before we head back."

Without a word, Joanie joined Wayne at the edge. He put his arm around her and adjusted her phone for the photo. He smiled at the camera, clicked the picture, and said, "Are we still on for our special dinner?"

"Oh, you better believe I'm holding you to that." Joanie looked at the picture he'd taken. "Your eyes were closed! Try it again. Look at the dot. Say cheese and keep your eyes open. I'm telling you, this is like working with a ninety-year-old." She jabbed him in the ribs and said, "I love you, old man."

22

"Where are we going?" Octavius said with Suzanne next to him in the backseat of the mayor's car as they flew down the highway, Timmy vaping in the front passenger seat.

"If it's okay with you, I think we should go to StoneSpell and get this figured out," Mars said, eyeing Octavius in the rearview mirror as he drove.

"Get what figured out?" said Suzanne, her right leg bouncing nonstop. "You said we were going back to your car."

"I do need my car," Octavius said, knowing he had to be very careful. He preferred to have time to think things through and plan before guests arrived at StoneSpell.

"I'll take you back to it," Mars said. "But . . . first things first."

Octavius wondered what on earth Mars had in mind?

Having a talk with Suzanne?

Worse?

Octavius ran down a checklist of precautions in his mind. He'd fed the ladies in the basement that morning and given them their daily dosages. "I suppose that will work," he said. "Timmy, please roll your window down if you insist on doing that in here."

"Get what figured out?" Suzanne repeated, louder. "What are you going to do, bury me in the backyard at StoneSpell because I found out you run a massive drug operation?"

The car hummed along in silence.

Slowly, Mars looked up into his rearview mirror again and glared at Octavius with deep lines carved into his forehead.

Octavius felt his face flush. The last thing he needed was Mars and Timmy getting too deeply involved in his affairs. If anything needed to be done about Suzanne, he could handle it without their intervention.

Tension hung in the air, which smelled like funnel cakes. Octavius put his face in the crook of his arm to breathe normal air.

"So, you're a drug dealer," Suzanne said to Octavius. "Would've been nice if you'd told me. Kind of an important detail to leave out."

Octavius put his large left hand over both of hers, which were freezing. She was having a cold flash, plus she was itching her eye, tapping her foot like a machine—and growing agitated. "We'll talk about this alone, okay?" he said.

"Why can't we talk about it right now?" she said. "There must've been a million pills up there. Where do they come from? Who do you sell them to? You know what you're doing to people?"

Suzanne's eyes filled with tears. "This is sick. *I'm* sick, but what do you care? It's all about *you*, isn't it?"

Octavius patted her hands and she shook them away. "Get off me," she spit. "I don't even know you." She looked away from him, out the window. "I don't even know myself anymore."

"Suzanne," Octavius whispered evenly, "let's not make a scene. I don't want to talk about this in front of Mars and Timmy. I will explain everything to you. Here . . ." He stuffed a hand in his coat pocket and produced two white pills—the infamous China White that may or may not be lethal. He grabbed his bottle of water from the cup holder and nudged her. "Take these."

He knew she couldn't resist a fresh bump.

Mars watched in the rearview.

Suzanne didn't even hesitate. She grabbed the pills, threw them into her mouth, and took a long swig from the plastic water bottle.

Octavius snickered to himself.

That'll take care of her for a while.

But she piped up. "Maybe when we get to StoneSpell you'll want to show these guys the basement," Suzanne said loudly. "They can see what you've been up to down there. That'll really blow their minds." She snickered and took another drink.

Octavius clenched his teeth and squeezed her arm as hard as he could.

"Ouch!" She spilled water all over the front of herself.

He gripped harder, like a tightening vice.

"Stop!" Suzanne yelled. "Get your hands off me!"

Timmy tilted his head straight back looking at the ceiling of the car and said, "Calm down back there, kiddos. We're almost there."

Suzanne gritted her teeth and punched Octavius in the arm repeatedly.

"Let me out of this car!" she yelled.

Octavius let go of her and straightened himself in the seat, brushing himself off as if his clothes had been covered in crumbs.

This is out of control.

This was *not* something he did—especially in the company of others.

He leveled his gaze at Suzanne and whispered, "We will talk about this *alone*."

Mars's phone rang loudly over the car speakers. "Everybody—quiet!" He examined the screen and put the phone up to his ear, which cut off the audio from the speakers.

"Maddox," he answered.

He listened intently.

He glanced at Timmy, then at Octavius in the rearview.

"Go on," he said.

Mars listened as he veered the car off the exit ramp in the vicinity of StoneSpell.

"Where in Nevada?" Mars said to the caller. He listened for another twenty seconds, then exploded, cursing a blue streak.

The outburst unsettled Octavius because Mars was usually cool. And Octavius did not like it at all that Mars mentioned Nevada, especially after what had happened to the girl in Las Vegas.

Octavius forced himself to take a deep breath, hold it, and exhale long and slow. He did so again, but his forehead prickled with sweat.

Things were unraveling by the second.

He had to keep his wits about him.

At least Suzanne had quieted down. She was staring out her window.

Mars lowered his voice with the caller. "What are the police saying and has there been an autopsy?"

Uh-oh. Not another death.

Suzanne snapped to attention. "Autopsy? What the heck is going on?"

Out the corner of his eye, Octavius could see that Suzanne was staring at him, but he looked straight ahead, waiting for Mars to finish the call.

"You can take me home!" Suzanne yelled. Then she turned away and mumbled something about getting straight.

That'll be the day.

Mars seethed and motioned wildly for Octavius to keep Suzanne quiet.

After another minute, Mars said, "Keep me updated." He ended the call, cussed, and slammed the phone down on the glossy wood console. He adjusted his rearview mirror, shook his head, and mouthed words to Octavius that he couldn't understand.

"Well, spill the beans," Suzanne said in an upbeat tone.

The car was silent.

Octavius thought if Suzanne kept talking, Mars would stop the car and strangle her.

Octavius and Timmy knew Mars would weigh his next words carefully in front of Suzanne.

"Someone die from your drugs?" Suzanne said.

Mars made a hard left turn as if to jolt Suzanne, followed by a sharp right into Octavius's neighborhood.

"We have a repeat of Las Vegas," Mars said.

"Where?" Timmy said.

"Carson City."

"Oh, so there's more than one!" Suzanne said. "This is great, just great. I'm not only dating a drug dealer, but one who's dealing toxic stuff." She laughed as if she was drunk and didn't care.

Mars leaned over and whispered something to Timmy.

Octavius burned with indignation.

How dare they . . . plan something without consulting me.

Timmy pulled back and stared at Mars. He then glanced back at

Suzanne, looked forward, and took another hit of his vape pipe. He exhaled a thick cloud of sweet smoke out the window, but most of it blew back in on Octavius.

Mars swung the Audi into the driveway at StoneSpell.

Octavius was furious with the whole situation. He needed to get out of the car and take control of matters.

The Audi jerked to a stop and Octavius reached for his door handle.

But before Mars even got the car in park, Timmy flew out his door in a flash and stood with both hands on his big gun—pointed directly at Octavius and Suzanne in the back seat.

23

AFTER RETURNING from the Roundabout Trail—and making a quick stop for a Starbucks—Joanie was bushed. She would try to call Suzanne later. She kicked off her shoes, pecked Wayne on the cheek, and wrapped up in a blanket on the bed at the tiny house for a nap. She closed her eyes and cleared her head, glad she'd burned some calories before their big dinner out.

It had been so good to see Wayne become more and more relaxed on the trip. His police work in Portland was all-consuming. He was such a hard worker, often putting in ten to sixteen hour days. It was dangerous—and his age concerned Joanie. He was still mentally sharp and in good physical condition, but anyone approaching sixty years old is simply more fragile than the younger cops.

How he would laugh if he ever heard me call him 'fragile.'

Joanie smiled, rolled onto her stomach, and got the pillow just right. She thought about how funny it was that she and Wayne kidded each other about getting old. *Thank God we're healthy . . . and the kids are healthy.* Because of her autism, daughter Leena would likely always be with them; that was something they'd accepted a long time ago—and had learned to embrace.

Joanie checked the time, 3:40 p.m., and closed her eyes. As she drifted off to sleep, thinking about Wayne and his job, she quietly thought, *Your will be done . . . Your will be done.*

She was asleep.

In a vivid dream, Octavius walked beside her, laughed, gave her a seductive smile, and reached out to take her hand.

She awoke with a start.

Her eyes flicked open wide.

Her heart pounded.

She remained still.

She looked around the light bedroom with its southwest décor of clay pottery, triangle mirrored wall hangings, turquoise candles, and Indian print pillows. There was even a little manger scene for Christmas.

She'd slept only twenty minutes and wondered what Suzanne was doing at that moment. Based on her talk with Suzanne's mom, Joanie was almost certain Suzanne had lied to her about going to Bend.

Why? Why would she make up the story about Uncle Steve having a heart attack? Would she lie to me so blatantly?

The only logical explanation was that Suzanne wanted to ditch Joanie.

That made her heart sick.

It also made her suspicious of Octavius.

She closed her eyes again. She wanted to forget about Suzanne and go back to sleep, because she wanted to be at her best for the dinner out with Wayne. But she doubted she was going to be able to get back to that restful state she was in a few minutes earlier.

She rolled onto her back, clasped her hands across her stomach, and stared up at the white ceiling. Leena would be at play practice about now. Brandon would probably be eating, playing video games, or hanging out with friends—until it was time to pick Leena up.

The door to the bedroom pushed open quietly.

Joanie looked over.

Wayne was standing there with his laptop open, crunching on a carrot.

"Not asleep?" he said.

"I slept. Got a hot date tonight." She wasn't about to tell him she'd dreamed about Octavius.

Wayne came into the room and sat on the bed next to her.

"After last night I had Virgil run Octavius through the database

—I called him this morning when you were at breakfast. Just heard back from him." Wayne lifted the laptop "He used the photo of Octavius, the one from his website, to run facial recognition. You were right."

Joanie shot up, pushed the blanket aside, and crossed her arms with a shiver.

Portland PD Investigator Virgil Bennett was one of Wayne's best friends and closest colleagues, and by 'database' Wayne was referring to the Oregon police database, LEDS: Law Enforcement Data Systems, which could find out virtually anything about anyone who'd been in trouble with the law.

"I can't get into the system from here, but Virgil sent a bunch of screenshots." Wayne shared the computer with Joanie, who was sitting up at full attention. "Want me to cut right to the chase or go from birth to now?" he said.

"Birth to now," Joanie said nervously.

Wayne took a bite of the carrot and started in.

"Frederick Oscar Hunter is his real name. Born in Pittsburgh. Arrested as a teen for vandalism of a church—slap on the wrist. Dropped out of a Catholic college in Pennsylvania, then moved around a lot. Worked at a pawn shop in Buffalo. Busted there for cocaine use, did thirty days. Arrested at a raid on a massage parlor in Baltimore—he was a customer, got no time for that because they were after the business owners."

"Slow down." Joanie was trying to process it all.

Wayne paused, then continued. "Went to an art school for a stint in Cincinnati where a female professor accused him of rape." Wayne glanced up at Joanie, shook his head, and continued. "He got off that charge for lack of evidence, moved to south Florida, and got a job at a fancy restaurant and yacht club in Boca Grande. He must've gotten married down there, because in 2010 he was charged with domestic violence, aggravated stalking, spent a night in jail, pled no contest, and was put on probation for six months."

Joanie's head dropped. Her whole body sighed. She was speechless.

"I'm assuming they got divorced, because there's no mention of her any more after that," Wayne said. "He had his own pool service business in Placida, Florida, and there he was busted for buying 'a large quantity' of illegal prescription drugs: oxycontin. He did five months in a Charlotte County prison."

"That's it. She's on pain killers!" Joanie exclaimed. "I bet you any money Suzanne's addicted to pain killers. That explains why she acted so weird around us, why she didn't show for dinner, why she was staggering into her place with him . . . why her mom thinks she's on drugs."

"Could be," Wayne shrugged. "We haven't even got to the juiciest part yet. He must've moved to St. Augustine in about 2015 or '16, as far as I can figure. Worked as a salesman for a big volume boat seller. Must've settled in there for a few years. Then—"

"Oh my word!" Joanie's hands shot to her mouth and her eyes bulged as she read ahead of Wayne and saw the mug shot of the missing woman.

"Yep," Wayne said. "Late 2017, Frederick Oscar Hunter was questioned *extensively* in the case of a missing woman." He tapped the photo of the attractive brunette with glistening brown eyes on his laptop. "Janine Sharp, thirty-three. A widow. Owned a high-end art gallery in Flagler Beach. They believe she was abducted from her luxury condo—no sign of forced entry."

Joanie shook her head in shock.

"They think it was someone she knew—and she knew Octavius," Wayne said. "She'd dated him several times. At one point, he inquired about selling some of his paintings at her gallery and she said no; they weren't good enough. That's what her brother said."

"I can't . . . I just can't digest this, Wayne," Joanie said. "I've got to warn Suzanne."

"During the investigation, Janine's older brother, Randy, said she'd been acting weird ever since she'd started seeing Octavius. Randy suspected Octavius all along. He believed drugs were involved and he was sure it was Octavius who abducted her. When the police finally gave up on Octavius, Randy assaulted him with a crowbar at the boat dealership in St. Augustine. Octavius got twenty-two stitches on his head—which explains the scar—and pressed charges. Randy had to do time for assault and battery."

"I bet you Suzanne doesn't know any of this," said Joanie, who was dizzy from all the information.

"He moved to Sedona not long after he was cleared of Janine Sharp's disappearance."

"Was she ever found?" Joanie's heart thundered.

"No." Wayne shook his head. "It's a cold case."

24

SUZANNE PRESSED down on her right leg, trying to get it to stop bouncing as she sat along the fireplace in Octavius's great room. Mars had ordered her to sit there. She knew if she didn't relax Octavius would figure out she hadn't taken the pills he'd given her in the car—and he would force her to take more. The men—Mars, Timmy, and Octavius—stood in a huddle in the kitchen thirty feet away, whispering in hushed, often heated exchanges.

Seeing the drug operation at DoughWorx had awakened Suzanne. It was as if a light switch had flipped and everything had come into vivid focus—namely, the fact that she was hopelessly addicted to pain killers and that Octavius was controlling her mind, her body, her whole life.

As she sat there awkwardly, like a child awaiting punishment, every muscle and bone in her body ached. She was cold and hot, cold and hot. For the tenth time she stopped herself from rocking back and forth and scratching herself like a crazy person. The men periodically looked over at her as they continued their intense discussion.

Suzanne could tell Octavius was on the defensive. Mars and Timmy were uptight, pointing fingers, getting up in Octavius's face. Suzanne was sure they were upset because she'd stumbled upon their drug operation. The question was, how serious was this? Timmy's gun was on the kitchen counter near him, along with her phone, which he'd taken from her when they'd gotten out of the car.

"She was *already* blabbing too much!" Mars said above a whisper, veins protruding from his neck. Octavius put his big hands up, as if to calm Mars, as if to assure him that he had the situation under control.

Suzanne wanted to give in. She wanted to take the two pills from her pocket that she'd spit back into her hand and swallow them now; she could do it without water. She reached down and touched her pants, felt the outline of the pills in her pocket. She wanted them desperately, because she knew they would make the trouble go away. They would make everything a breeze again—even this mess.

But not now. Not this time.

This was *real*.

These men were bad.

She must think clearly.

She needed to get her hands on a phone so she could call 911. It crossed her mind to try to reach Joanie because her husband was a cop, but she couldn't bring them into this—it was too dangerous. Besides, Octavius had no landlines in the house. It was her phone or no phone.

Her best plan was probably to run.

The word 'basement' was spoken loudly among the men in the form of a question.

They fell silent.

Timmy slowly turned and looked at Suzanne, followed by Mars's gaze.

Octavius did not look at her but continued staring at the other men.

"What's in the basement, Suzanne?" Mars called and took several steps toward her. "What's he hiding?"

Suzanne's body tensed. She swallowed hard and felt her face warm.

Octavius finally looked at her and shook his head ever so slightly as if to tell her to keep her mouth shut.

Suzanne had a split-second decision to make—tell Mars and Timmy about the women in the basement and take her chances on how they would respond, or keep Octavius's secret, hope the men would leave, and figure out how to get away from Octavius when she was alone with him.

"No idea what you're talking about," Suzanne said, then awaited the fallout.

"*You said* he had something going on down there. *What?*" Timmy blasted, snatching his gun from the counter and slipping Suzanne's phone in his back pocket.

Suzanne shook her head and held her hands up. "Sorry. I honestly can't remember."

"Get over here!" Timmy waved the gun at Suzanne.

"We'll all go down and see." Mars reached around his back and pulled out a revolver of his own. He nudged it toward Octavius. "Lead the way."

Octavius shrugged and told them again he had nothing to hide, but did what he was told.

As they reached the steps and made their way down in silence, Suzanne felt like throwing up. She'd seen the opioid operation and was an obvious threat. The question was, were Mars and Timmy killers? *Timmy could be—he had the eyes and temperament.* She feared she may not return up those steps alive.

They reached the lower level and Octavius pointed out a bathroom, a simple but luxurious spare bedroom, followed by a game room across the hall filled with several pinball machines, a ping pong table, foosball table, a billiards table, and a large screen TV mounted to the wall and surrounded by three spacious couches.

"What's in there?" Timmy pointed to a bronze-colored metal door toward the end of the hall. Suzanne had never been in that room before, or at least she thought she hadn't. She wondered if that's where the other women could be. Maybe she had been in there after all.

Octavius coughed, mumbled something about "security," and walked toward it. He pushed it open and went into the dark room. The others followed.

"Holy . . ." Timmy exclaimed as he stepped in and looked in awe at an entire wall filled with glowing color monitors showing various rooms and common areas throughout StoneSpell.

Suzanne's stomach churned with a mix of acid and foreboding.

Beneath the monitors was a huge desk featuring two large computers and several laptops. "What is this place?" Timmy said.

Suzanne wondered the same thing.

"Security," Octavius said in a nonchalant tone. "There are cameras throughout StoneSpell. These are the monitors for those cameras." He mumbled something more about "protection" and "can't be too careful."

Mars and Timmy looked closely from monitor to monitor.

Suzanne did the same, wondering what kind of pervert she'd been dating? The monitors showed the great room where she'd just been sitting by the fireplace several minutes earlier, the kitchen, garage, patio, deck, pool, hot tub, front foyer . . . Suzanne could feel her heart ticking rapidly.

Octavius stood in silence with his arms crossed, not making eye contact with Suzanne.

One screen showed Octavius's master bedroom.

Suzanne's blood ran cold.

She noticed two separate monitors off to the side. She did a doubletake. Her right hand covered her mouth. The monitor showed her apartment—and bedroom!

"I'm gonna be sick." She dashed from the room.

"Stop!" Timmy called.

She didn't care.

She made it to the small bathroom down the hall, slid to her knees, and threw up in the toilet. She slammed the toilet paper roll, ripped off a long piece, and wiped her mouth, breathing hard, sweating. She ripped off another five feet of toilet paper and wiped her forehead and face.

"You didn't take the oxy he gave you." Timmy said, standing in the doorway of the bathroom, gun in hand.

Suzanne got to her knees, flushed, leaned on the toilet, and caught her breath. "Leave me alone," she said.

"You saw upstairs at DoughWorx." He took a hit of his pipe, put his shoulders back, and held in the fumes as long as he could before letting out a thick cloud of vape with a small cough.

She looked up at him and nodded. "Yeah, but I'm not going to say anything. It doesn't have anything to do with me. Just let me go. Honestly, I couldn't care less about what you guys do."

Timmy laughed. "Come on, get up."

She was slow to her feet and trembling. And freezing cold.

"Yeah, you're withdrawing." He pointed with his gun for her to go.

"Please, don't say anything." Slowly, she led the way back to the dark room with the glowing monitors and they entered.

Mars was standing to the far right, closely examining one of the screens. "Where's this?" He tapped the monitor and swiveled his head toward Octavius.

Suzanne squinted at the screen to which Mars was referring.

Oh no.

Her legs almost went out from under her. Her head spun. She gripped the chair at the desk and stared at it for a moment until everything came back into focus.

She looked up at the room on the monitor. It was dark with a blueish tint to it, but there was no doubt it was the room where she'd been kept the night Joanie and Wayne had been at StoneSpell—the room with the two other women.

Octavius only stared at Mars with his mouth hanging open.

"What is that?" Timmy made his way toward the screen. Mars stepped back and Timmy squinted at the monitor. "Are those beds? And are there *people* in those beds? What the heck is this, Big O? Are those women?" Timmy cackled like a maniac, turned, looked at Suzanne and said in a high voice, "You know about this?"

Suzanne shook her head and glared at Octavius. But he stood with his arms crossed, not looking at her, rocking on his toes.

"Where is it?" Mars said in a low, serious tone as he loosened his pink tie.

"It has nothing to do with you so leave it alone," Octavius finally said. "Nothing to do with us or our partnership."

"Just like she doesn't?" Mars flicked his revolver toward Suzanne.

Timmy jabbed a finger at the monitor. "Show us that room—right now."

"I won't." Octavius let his large hands drop to his sides and breathed in deeply through his nose, his broad shoulders setting back. "That has absolutely zero to do with our situation. Why don't you two be on your way? You have my word our affairs will remain completely confidential." He nodded toward Suzanne. "We're going to have a chat when you go, and Suzanne won't be saying anything to anyone about DoughWorx." He fixed his eyes on her and said, "Will you?"

Suzanne shook her head vehemently, her pulse pounding. "I'm not saying anything. I promise. I don't care. It doesn't matter to me. I just want to . . . to go about my life." Her teeth chattered as she spoke, and she could barely breathe. With a trembling hand she felt for the pills in her pocket, wanting them desperately.

Mars walked over to within a foot of Octavius and spoke while looking down at the floor. "Let me make this perfectly clear. We're not going anywhere till we find out who these people are and how much they know. If you're telling the truth, fine." He glanced at Suzanne. "Then we'll only have one problem to eliminate."

25

Deetz adjusted the collar of his white dress shirt and the knot of his navy tie while looking in the bathroom mirror. He liked how the sun had splashed his face with color—a cross between sunburn and tan. A bit of sun on the cheeks always made him look younger. He was almost ready to go, just needed to clean his glasses, get a shot of cologne, and grab the sport coat he'd brought along solely for this occasion.

He ducked his head into the bedroom. Joanie still wasn't in there yet.

"Come on, babe," he yelled. "You need to get ready."

He heard her yell something back that he couldn't understand.

Deetz had read about The Mainstay restaurant online before they'd even made the trip. It was a small five-star, fine-dining bistro tucked in the foothills of Sedona's Red Rock Mountains that specialized in a mouthwatering dish called lamb adobo. The head chef was known nationwide. Deetz planned to order champagne, appetizers, the whole works. He really wanted it to be a special night for Joanie, who said she'd brought along a new "Barbie dress" just in case they did something special.

She came in the bedroom in a hurry, cradling the open laptop.

"I know exactly what I'm wearing. I'll be ready in a flash. But you've got to hear this." She plopped down on the bed and examined the screen, about to start reading something.

"We have a reservation, you know," he said.

"I know, I know. I won't make us late. But, I have to tell you this. Suzanne told me at breakfast that the first time she met Octavius was right after she'd had a tooth extracted. She said she was all bruised and swollen, and that she was on pain meds, but she said she had to get out of the house. She went to an art show in Jessup and met Octavius at his art booth for the first time. I bet you any money that's when she got hooked."

Wayne mulled it over, antsy for her to start getting ready. "Possible I guess."

"Octavius did prison time for buying a large quantity of oxycontin. He took advantage of her."

"Okay, I hear you. You may be onto something. Can you get ready while we talk, please?"

"Hold on, let me read this to you, then I'll get ready—I promise."

He sighed audibly and she kept going.

"*Anyone* who takes opioids is at risk of developing addiction and *women* may have biological tendencies to become dependent on prescription pain relievers more quickly than men." Joanie read quickly as she sat cross-legged on the bed, rigid, hunched over the glowing screen. "Opioids are highly addictive because they activate powerful reward centers in the brain. They trigger the release of endorphins, your brain's feel-good neurotransmitters. Endorphins muffle your perception of pain and boost feelings of pleasure, creating a temporary but powerful sense of well-being."

"Okay, okay, they're addictive, I get it," Wayne said.

"Keep listening, please. Symptoms can include initial euphoria followed by apathy, slowed cognition and movement, chronic scratching, clouded thinking . . ." She closed the laptop dramatically and leaned over it toward Wayne. "That's Suzanne. That's *exactly* the way she's acting." Her mouth and eyes were wide open, waiting for a response.

Joanie was probably right. Suzanne could well be addicted to pain killers. And Octavius may even be supplying them. But at that moment, Wayne was anxious to make it to the restaurant on time. He'd been looking forward to this romantic night for weeks. He'd had it up to his ears with Suzanne and Octavius. For now, all he wanted to do was take his wife out for a nice dinner where they could concentrate on each other.

Joanie tossed the laptop on the bed and started taking her shoes and socks off. "Well . . . what do you think?"

"You might be right," Wayne said, throwing on his jacket. "You better hurry."

Joanie stripped down to her underwear and went into the small bathroom. Everything in the tiny house was close together. She splashed water on her face, dried off with a towel, and leaned over the sink to do her makeup.

"What can we do about it?" she glanced at him.

"Nothing—tonight," Wayne said.

Joanie dropped her arms and gave him an exasperated glare. "My gosh, Wayne, you're being really selfish right now."

"Honey," he looked at his watch, "we have a dinner reservation in like twenty-five minutes. It's going to take fifteen to get there, at least. I don't want to be in a big rush, and I don't want us to be late. Can we focus on us tonight?"

Joanie started back in on her makeup. "Of course, but she needs to know all the stuff we've found out."

Wayne took in a deep breath and told himself to be calm or he would ruin the evening. "Maybe tomorrow we can try to see her, if she really is still here."

"Will you really do that with me?" she pleaded.

"Yes. Now, come on."

"I figure since she told me she was going to Bend she probably won't be at her place; she'll want to make it look like she's gone." Joanie threw her makeup into a bag and headed for the closet in the bedroom.

Wayne could tell she was pleased he'd agreed to try to find Suzanne the next day, which he realized he would very likely regret.

Joanie slipped a tiny black dress over her head and adjusted it in the mirror. The dress had a square, low cut front and long, lace sleeves. "Can you zip me?"

"Gladly." He zipped up the back but couldn't see the tiny hook "Hold on." He took his glasses off, held them in his mouth, and leaned in about four inches from the little hook at the top of the zipper.

"Having a hard time there, gramps?" she said.

He laughed. "I got it, I got it."

He turned her around to face him.

He put his glasses back on and looked her up and down. "You look beautiful."

"It's about as good as it's going to get." She went over to the small dresser and dug around in another bag. "Silver or pearls?" She held up a silver earring to one ear and a pearl earring up to the other.

"Silver," he said.

She nodded and hurried to put on the earrings, followed by a matching necklace.

"You wearing a jacket?" he said.

She threw on some black high heels, eyed herself in the mirror, ran her fingers over her dark eyebrows, and patted the silver necklace. "I don't really have a coat that matches. You think I'll be okay without?"

"Maybe put the fleece one around you in the car and just go in without it?"

Joanie winked, clicked her tongue, and pointed at him with her fingers in the shape of a gun. "Good plan, good plan."

26

As Octavius began walking down the basement hallway with the others behind him, slowly as possible toward the sleek wood staircase—and the hidden chamber beyond it—a hundred thoughts raced through his rattled mind.

First, he was an *utter fool* to have allowed himself to be wrangled into the current crucible in which he found himself. If he ended up dying within the next few minutes—which was feasible based on what he was tentatively planning—he supposed he deserved it.

Second, Suzanne was now dead to him. If Mars and Timmy showed mercy (and he doubted they would) and let her live, Octavius would be the one who would be forced to—dispose of her. It was indeed an unpleasant thought, but he would have to embrace it if he wanted the flourishing partnership with Mars and Timmy to continue. And he certainly did, because that was the only way he could continue living in opulence at StoneSpell and to continue to nurture his persona as a burgeoning artist, entrepreneur, and local celebrity.

Nothing and no one will stand in the way of that.

Octavius could tell by the way Suzanne was bouncing and scratching and sweating that she hadn't taken the pills he'd given her in the car. Perhaps seeing the drug operation sobered her up and made her want to get straight. That didn't much matter to him now. If it did come down to him getting rid of her, he would make sure she was good and high before he did the deed.

He would prefer to keep Suzanne alive. In fact, the thought of adding her to his growing stable of lady friends sent a shiver of delight up his spine. But deep down he knew Mars and Timmy would not believe he could keep Suzanne quiet if they let her live.

"Hurry it up, Big O," Timmy said from behind.

They were almost to the staircase.

Third, Octavius had a momentous decision to make within about five seconds and that was—should he go for the gun that was hidden beneath the second step of the staircase and turn it on Mars and Timmy? It was cocked, loaded, and mounted there for precisely such an occasion as this.

Ingenious.

As he came to a stop at the staircase, Octavius surmised that he did not believe for one fleeting moment that Mars or Timmy would keep their mouths shut about the two women behind the steps—and that would eventually lead to his demise.

"Here we are," Octavius announced and turned to face Mars, Timmy, and Suzanne—whose skin was the color of a priest's collar. "This is a secret staircase. So, before you go getting all trigger happy, just know that I am about to bend down and lift up this lower half of the stairs. It's on hydraulic lifts—"

"You gotta be kidding me." Timmy chuckled into a fist.

Octavius continued. "We will then walk beneath it to a door, behind which is the scene you noted on the monitor in question. All clear?"

As Octavius bent down, grabbed the bottom step and began lifting—careful to use his knees—his mind blanked with uncertainty.

With an oily hissing sound, the set of lower steps began to rise.

"Un-be-lievable," Timmy said in awe.

Octavius pulled the bottom of the staircase up to his waist, then up to his chest, above his head. The instant it locked into place he grabbed the big gun from its brackets—pleased with how easily it freed itself—whipped around and blasted Timmy in the chest.

Everything blurred into slow motion.

The gunshot rang in Octavius's ears.

A wisp of smoke.

Timmy leaving his feet, catapulting backward, crumpling to the floor.

Suzanne's bloodcurdling scream.

The smell of gunpowder.

Blood splatter on the wall.

Mars frozen in shock with his mouth wide open and his little gun to his side.

Events kicked back into normal speed and, with his ears still ringing, Octavius trained the weapon on Mars.

"Don't! No!" Mars cowered. "Please, Octavius, don't shoot, don't shoot! We can work all this out."

Suzanne was on the floor, her arms covering her head, her body shaking violently.

Octavius looked down at Timmy and said, "I knew he would never keep my secret." His eyes flicked back up to Mars. "What about you, mayor? How good are you at keeping secrets?"

27

As J OANIE and Wayne stepped into the dark foyer of The Mainstay restaurant, Joanie shook off the cold, having left her jacket in the car, and her senses were instantly delighted by the romantic dim lighting, quiet chatter of patrons, clinking of silverware to dishes, and appetizing aroma.

A tall young blond hostess wearing a large oval turquoise necklace nodded, smiled brightly, said she'd been expecting them, and began to escort them to their table. As Joanie followed, they weaved through an already packed upscale dining room featuring fine china and white linen napkins, smiling dinner guests with faces glowing from the candles between them, and an array of mouthwatering entrees.

A roar went up to Joanie's left. The loud laughter and talk came from a high-end bar appointed with dark woods and leather furniture and, more specifically, from a sitting area where four women were gathered around a table that was littered with carafes of wine, bottles of bourbon and tequila, and glasses of all shapes and sizes, including shot glasses. Each of the women wore a fine dress or pantsuit with expensive jewelry, makeup, and hair. One, about thirty-five with dark hair and auburn streaks, looked familiar. Joanie wondered if she may be a famous actress or celebrity. The group looked—and sounded—as if they'd been there awhile, drinking heavily.

The hostess seated Joanie and Wayne at a small candlelit table near a roaring fireplace, handed them large menus, and told them their server, Dawson, would be with them shortly. The fireplace mantel was centered by a large wreath and laced with tiny white lights and Christmas greenery.

Joanie found it so romantic whenever Wayne took the initiative to find a nice restaurant and make a reservation without telling her.

Soft jazz played all around them.

Another whoop went up from the ladies in the bar, bordering on obnoxious.

"They're having a good time," Wayne said.

"Yeah, it looked like they'd been at it awhile. Did you see them?"

"No, I was too busy looking at everyone's plates. Did you see the ribs?"

"No, I was too busy looking at the table of women in the bar; they are blitzed. One of them looked familiar. I just can't place her."

"Sure, sure," Wayne said.

Joanie sat up as high as she could in her chair and leaned to one side, trying to see into the bar. "Actually, I can see them from here."

"Don't stare, honey."

"Can you see them sitting around the table in there? Four women?"

Reluctantly, Wayne turned around and looked toward the bar area.

"Yep."

"Does the one in the white dress look familiar at all? I think she's an actress."

"Hmm."

Dawson, a thin young man with black hair, freckles, and a protruding Adam's apple introduced himself and asked if they'd dined there before. He wore black pants, a white dress shirt, and an off-white tie.

"No, but we've heard great things," Wayne said, eyeing the wine list.

"Very good," Dawson said. "May we start you off with a cocktail and an appetizer? A local favorite is the fried goat cheese with pear, prosciutto, and balsamic reduction."

Joanie raised her eyebrows. It sounded scrumptious.

Wayne knew Joanie loved anything with prosciutto. He looked up at Dawson and smiled. "That sounds marvelous. We'll have that and two glasses of the Cava champagne."

"Excellent choice, sir." Dawson disappeared without writing anything down.

"Wow," Joanie said, "aren't you Mister Wine-and-Dine." She was truly impressed.

Wayne shrugged and smiled. "You deserve a nice dinner out. I did a little research. The Cava champagne is from some sort of unique Spanish grapes."

"Mmm, sounds delish."

"It smells so good in here," he said.

"This is so nice. Thank you, honey."

Wayne looked into her eyes. "You're welcome. I love you, babe. You look beautiful tonight. You're getting tan."

A woman's voice spoke loudly from the bar, almost a yell, followed by screaming laughter. Many patrons in the restaurant looked toward the bar, shook their heads in quiet disgust, whispered to each other. The outburst was obviously jolting and out of place for such a fine establishment.

Dawson showed up and presented their flute glasses of white bubbly. "Your appetizer will be ready momentarily," he said before dashing away.

Wayne lifted his glass and Joanie followed suit.

"Here's to our future," he said. "May God find favor on us and our loved ones. May he guide our decisions—and always give us wisdom. Cheers."

"Cheers," Joanie said as they clinked glasses, then sipped. "Mmm."

"Good stuff," Wayne said. "So, what are your big hopes and dreams for tomorrow? Are you going to take me on another big hiking adventure? Joanie's boot camp continues?"

She laughed.

Actually, she had planned to spend quite a bit of time with Suzanne on the trip, but since she'd supposedly left town, Joanie and Wayne had more time than expected together.

"What about those pink Jeep rides?" she said.

His face turned sour. "Are you kidding me? Those things go like straight up the mountains." He pointed a flattened hand at a ninety-degree angle.

"Oh, come on. They probably have mild, medium, and dangerous rides," she said.

"No, thanks. I feel the same way about those as I do about roller coasters—not fun."

"I'll go by myself," she kidded.

"Be my guest. I'll get the benefit from your life insurance."

"Very funny, mister. You wouldn't know what to do without me."

He covered her right hand with his.

They looked into each other's eyes and both smiled.

She was overwhelmed with thankfulness and tears pushed up to her eyes.

Wayne could probably tell she was trying not to cry and changed the subject. "What looks good to you for your entrée? You know the specialty is lamb adobo."

Joanie laughed and sniffed and dabbed her eyes with her napkin. "You've only mentioned that about a thousand times."

They both laughed, squeezed hands, and sipped their champagne.

"I passed a plate of ribs on the way in and they looked incredible," he said. "But I think I better have the lamb adobo. That's what I came for."

Dawson arrived and showed the appetizer as if he was presenting parents with a newborn baby. The fancy plate contained four ovals of fried cheese, each topped with pear and prosciutto, and the whole thing drizzled with brown sauce. They dug in and found the food to be utterly mouthwatering.

They reminisced about all the family vacations they'd taken—to the beach, Canada, the mountains, the Grand Canyon. They laughed about the one and only family camping trip when it thunder stormed the whole time and Leena got sick all night in the tent. They talked about how physically draining parenting had been when the kids were little and, at times, how mentally exhausting it was as they'd grown to be adults. They agreed it had all been worth it.

When Dawson came back around, Joanie ordered the ribs and Wayne stayed true to his word and went with the lamb.

A small, jolly man in a brown suit entered the dining room from the kitchen, opened the screen in front of the fireplace, and tossed on two fresh logs. He poked at the fire until he was happy with it, closed the screen, and left the room—smiling and nodding at guests as he went.

Joanie told Wayne she needed to use the ladies room before their food arrived. Just then, laughter arose again from the bar. Joanie leaned to look. The four women were standing, posing for a picture, which was being taken on one of their phones by a waiter they must have flagged down.

The instant the camera flashed and lit up their faces, Joanie recognized the woman in the white dress.

"Oh my word, Wayne, I know who that is now," she whispered excitedly.

"Nicole Kidman?" he said.

"It's the mayor's wife, the mayor of Jessup," Joanie said. "Marsden Maddox. I think her name is Candace."

Wayne nonchalantly turned around to look. "Yep, you're right."

"How do you know?"

"I saw a picture at Octavius's house. I snooped for a second before using the restroom. She was in the picture."

"Yeah, they're really good friends with Octavius and Suzanne. I read all about it online."

"Okay, we solved the mystery. Now, let's forget about it and enjoy our dinner."

Joanie gently pushed her chair back and stood. "Okay, I'm going to the restroom. Back in a flash."

"Dear, don't you dare say anything to her."

Joanie smiled, brushed the front of her dress, and made her way toward the bar, where she assumed the restroom would be. As she approached the area where the four women were still standing after having had their picture taken, she went directly up to Candace Maddox.

"Excuse me, do you know where the restrooms are?"

Candace, whose lips and cheeks looked freshly injected with

Botox, looked Joanie up and down, then sloshed her drink toward the back of the bar. "That way," she said in a demeaning tone.

"Thanks." Joanie started to head in that direction, but stopped and turned back toward Candace. "Excuse me, again. Sorry. But you look so familiar. You wouldn't happen to be Mayor Maddox's wife?"

With that acknowledgement, Candace's cold expression disappeared, her shoulders and head set back, she flashed a celebrity smile, and stuck her hand out. "Candace Maddox."

Joanie shook Candace's hand, which felt wet and coated with lotion.

"Joanie Deetz," she said. "Here on vacation from Portland. I'm actually friends with someone you know—Octavius Hunt."

Candace's head wavered like a bobble head doll. "Really? Small world, right?" Her breath smelled strongly of booze and she swayed when she spoke.

Joanie was thinking Candace would have no recollection of their conversation the next day.

"Actually, I just met Octavius for the first time," Joanie said. "I'm really lifelong friends with his girlfriend, Suzanne."

Candace's shoulders dropped and her plastic face went sour. "Oh, well in that case." She slurred her words and started to walk away. Then she erupted in sloppy laughter and turned back toward Joanie. "I'm just playing with you. Oc-ta-viush is a dear friend. Suzanne, well . . . we like her somewhat, too." She cackled again and took another swig of her drink. Her voice made her sound much older than she looked.

Joanie forced an awkward smile and was about to continue on to the restroom.

"Have you *seen* Suzanne?" Candace said, her head bobbing as if on puppet strings.

"Uh, yes," Joanie said. "I had breakfast with her—"

"What'd you think?" Candace tottered. "Was she flyin' high?"

"I'm sorry?" Joanie said, somewhat miffed.

"I mean, I feel bad for her. But it's *so* obvious." Candace looked around to make sure her friends couldn't hear her. When she did, she almost fell over. She stepped closer to Joanie. "Oc-ta-viush is a bad boy. He's hit on me before. Can you believe that? Mars has no idea. If he did, he'd kill him."

Joanie was speechless.

"Suzanne's got it pretty bad for the hillbilly heroin, right?" Candace said. "Everyone knows. How can you not notice."

"I thought . . . I thought something was wrong," Joanie said, realizing that if she wanted any more information out of Candace, now was the time to ask because the skids were greased.

"Ya think?" Candace said. "She needs to check herself into rehab, but good luck with that. Oc-ta-viush wouldn't have it." Candace leaned over and whispered into Joanie's ear. "He's behind it. I'm sure she's not the first."

Joanie's blood ran cold.

"You look surprised," Candace slurred. "I shouldn't have opened my big mouth. Sorry, not sorry." She laughed.

Joanie shook her head. "It's okay. I thought something was wrong. I couldn't put my finger on it."

"Who knows what they're up to out at StoneSpell. I don't really give a rip. I'm having a good time with my friends. True friends. Here," Candace put an arm around Joanie, "let me introduce you to my true friends right over here."

Joanie stood her ground and pulled back, making Candace's arm fall away. "What's happening at StoneSpell?" Joanie said. "Right now, you mean?"

"Big pow-wow. Mars, Oc-ta-viush, Suzanne, and a guy named Timmy Kondore." Candace spoke exaggeratedly, opened her eyes wide, then threw back the rest of her drink and crunched the ice loudly in her mouth. "Mars called from his car a while ago, said something came up they had to take care of out there. Fine. I'll just drink with my friends and run up a ginormous tab—maybe that'll get the big shot mayor's attention."

28

SUZANNE FELT as if she herself had been shot.

The blast from Octavius's gun blared in her ears.

Her energy leaked away from her like water going through a sieve.

Her head seemed to float ten feet above her aching body, which had dropped to the floor with the alarming shot that killed Timmy Kondore. His still body and the bloody mess on the wall couldn't possibly be real—but they were.

This was Suzanne's pitiful life.

Between the shock and the withdrawal symptoms—mainly deep muscle and bone pain—Suzanne knew more than ever that she needed help. She needed to get out of that house.

She needed God to intervene.

But she'd abandoned him.

She'd lied to Joanie.

She'd been dating a monster who'd drugged her daily, taken advantage of her mind and body—and now had committed cold-blooded murder.

"Don't do it." She could barely hear her own words, spoken to Octavius as he pointed the gun at Mars. "Stop it. Just stop." She was weak, so weak. Her hand trembled violently as she held it out to him. "Please. No more." She dropped back to the floor.

Octavius looked down at her, paused, and with one giant stride snatched the small revolver from Mars's hand. "You're going to get rid of Timmy's body and clean this up, now," Octavius ordered Mars.

Mars was nodding dramatically in agreement before Octavius had finished speaking.

"You're an accomplice to this." Octavius nodded toward Timmy. "And that will seal our partnership. Go on. Don't just stand there. Get your people in here or however you're going to do this. Hurry up."

The tan had drained completely from Mars's face. He, too, seemed in utter shock. He spoke in monotone. "I have a guy, Raymond G. He'll come in, take care of everything. Dispose of the body so it will never be found, clean this up as if it never happened. It will cost. But it will be worth it."

"Make the call," Octavius said, impatiently.

"Then what?" Mars said, pulling up a suspender that had fallen down. "We need to think this through."

"Then we go on with business as usual. I *have* thought it through. Now let's get on with this!"

Suzanne had locked in on the fact that her phone was in dead Timmy's back pocket. She needed to get it to call the police.

Mars wiggled his own phone in his thick hand. "I don't keep his number on this phone—in case I ever get taken in." He looked down at Timmy's lifeless body and back to Octavius. "It's on a burner at home—"

Octavius cussed and clenched a fist.

"Candace has it on her phone," Mars quickly responded.

Octavius pointed his gun at Mars's phone. "What are you waiting for? Call her."

Then he leveled his gaze at Suzanne, still sprawled out on the floor. "And you, young lady, you didn't take your pills, did you? Tsk, tsk, tsk."

Suzanne's face burned with fear and rage.

"We need to remedy that right now," Octavius said. "I know you want it."

She *did* want it! More than anything. But there was a corpse five feet from her. She knew she had to stay straight—or she could be incriminated or even killed herself.

I've got to get out of here.

Suzanne's eyes flicked frantically from Timmy's pocket, to Mars, to Octavius.

"Oh, Suzanne, something's going on in that pretty head of yours," Octavius said. He glanced at Mars, who was fumbling with his phone, then tilted his head and looked past the lifted staircase toward the bronze-colored metal door, then back at Suzanne. "I think it's time for you to take a long rest."

"So, you're saying Suzanne's still in Sedona?" Joanie said to drunk Candace in the dark bar at The Mainstay. "She told me she was flying to Oregon today to be with a sick relative."

"Oh, dang, my contact is screwed up." Candace bent over and probed a finger around in her right eye. "I swear I'm getting Lasik. Come over here for a second. I gotta set my drink down."

Candace left Joanie for the table where her friends were standing. Several men had gathered around them and they were all chatting lightheartedly.

Joanie looked over toward Wayne, who threw his hands up in the air as if to say, "What are you doing?" Luckily, their food hadn't arrived yet. Joanie followed Candace to find out all she could about the so-called "pow-wow" at StoneSpell.

The people standing around the table welcomed Candace back and noticed Joanie following her over.

"This is my friend Joanie." Candace slammed her glass on the messy table and began rummaging through her big floppy leather purse. "Joanie, these are all my friends. Hold on. I gotta find my drops."

Joanie smiled and shyly acknowledged everyone. One of the men was holding a piece of mistletoe over a woman's head, trying to get a kiss from her. Luckily, the group pretty much stuck to their conversations and didn't introduce themselves.

Candace stood up from her purse, threw her head back, fought to keep her balance, and squeezed about six eyedrops in her right eye; most of them missing and shooting down her face. She cursed, grabbed a napkin, and patted her face and eye.

"Sorry about that," she said to Joanie. "I've been telling Mars for a year I want Lasik, but he doesn't think it's advanced enough yet. Heck with that, I'm getting it." She blinked and adjusted the contact again with a finger to her eye then looked at Joanie and said, "My makeup okay?"

Joanie pointed to her left eye. "It's running a little right there."

Candace dabbed it and looked at Joanie for a response.

"All good," Joanie said.

"Good. Thanks. You want a drink?" As Joanie said no, Candace leaned over and poured herself three fingers of bourbon and stood back up with a sway.

She can't be driving. Probably has a limo.

"So, you think Suzanne is at StoneSpell now?" Joanie said. "She told me—"

"I know she is. Mars called from his car. She was with him. So were Octavius and Timmy." Candace sipped her drink. "Em, that's the good stuff. Sure you don't want a splash? Who're you here with anyway?"

"My husband. He's sitting over there." Joanie pointed but Candace didn't even look. "In fact, I need to get back."

"Candace." A tall brunette woman spoke loudly. "Candace!"

Candace turned toward her.

The woman pointed to Candace's purse. "Your phone."

Candace cursed, said "Sorry," clinked her glass on the table with a splash, and dug around in her bag, which pulsed and glowed with the sound of Pitbull's "Fireball." She finally found the phone, stood up, and answered.

"What? What for? What's going on, Mars?" Candace said, annoyed, then listened.

Joanie caught Wayne's eye and held up a finger to let him know she would be back in a second.

"Don't yell at me, Mars!" Candace spoke into the phone. "Fine, I don't really care what you do. It just better not backfire. Hold on." Shaking her head with clenched teeth, Candace took the phone away from her ear, examined the glowing screen, worked the buttons rapidly with her thumbs, then put it back to her ear. "I just texted his info. Did you get it?"

She nodded with a sour look on her face. "Don't expect me

home anytime soon. And I'm getting Lasik!" She jabbed a button to end the call, tossed the phone in her purse, grabbed her drink, and took a swig. She winced as the gulp burned her throat.

"SOS at StoneSpell," Candace said to Joanie, having difficulty pronouncing all the Ss. Candace shrugged her shoulders and took another sip. "I don't care anymore. I couldn't care less. Do what you need to do." She was talking to herself now.

"What's wrong?" Joanie said. "What's going on at StoneSpell?"

"Don't know the dirty details, but I can tell you this—when Raymond G gets involved, it's never good."

Alarms blared in Joanie's head. "Who's Raymond G?"

Candace craned her neck toward Joanie and locked eyes with her, her head bobbing unintentionally. Candace paused and blinked and contemplated before she finally spoke.

"If you're a friend of Suzanne's, you need to tell her to get the heck out of there, *now*." Candace put a finger to her lips and wobbled. "You didn't hear it from me."

29

AFTER MARS GOT through to Raymond G, "the cleaner," and assured Octavius the mystery man would arrive at StoneSpell within ninety minutes, Octavius left Mars in the basement and took Suzanne upstairs. It was dark out and the house had a chill, so he kicked up the heat and had Suzanne take a seat in the booth off the kitchen. He got crushed ice from the fridge, crossed to the bar, filled his glass with gin, and topped it off with a splash of organic lime tonic. He meandered toward Suzanne, drank deeply, and assessed matters.

Suzanne was draped over the table with her head and arms laying there, a soft glowing light shining from above. She moved restlessly with an occasional groan. Her body had become so used to regular heavy doses of pain killers, it was crying out for them now in the form of aches and pains, cold flashes, and occasional uncontrollable leg movements.

For Octavius it had become clear that things were over with Suzanne. It had been a good run, but between her seeing the drug operation at DoughWorx and watching him gun down Timmy Kondore—it was time to part ways. The question was, what to do with her?

For the short-term, he could drug her heavily and add her to his stable in the basement, but for the long-term that would not be a good solution. After all, Suzanne was an extremely smart woman. If she made up her mind to stop taking the drugs, he believed she may just have the chutzpah to pull it off.

That would not be good.

Octavius took another drink then found the extra-strength Tylenol in the kitchen and gave Suzanne three of them with a glass of water.

Suzanne squinted up at him then examined the pills on the table.

"It's just Tylenol," he said. "It'll take the edge off."

She tossed the pills into her mouth and drained all the water he'd put in the glass. She leaned back in the booth and stared at Octavius, her left leg bumping up and down like a piston.

As he self-medicated with the gin, Octavius's mind took him to a very dark place. He could offer to pay Raymond G extra—probably a lot extra—and have him take Suzanne with him. Just be done with her.

What a relief that would be.

Of course, that would mean Mars would know about it.

For all that matter, Octavius could have Raymond G take Mars along, too!

Octavius chuckled to himself, took another swig, and got serious. He couldn't simply make everyone disappear. If the mayor of Jessup vanished, it would be national news and Octavius couldn't afford that kind of attention. He had too many skeletons in his closet.

No, he needed to play this wisely and with as little ruckus as possible.

"Let me go." Suzanne's voice surprised Octavius. "Take me home or let me Uber. I promise I won't say anything to anyone."

Octavius walked over to her and groaned as he slid into the booth across from her.

"You're scared of me now, aren't you?" he said.

"This isn't about you." She set her shoulders back and inhaled deeply, then let out a long slow exhale. "I just want to get better."

He smiled briefly and nodded.

"Today has been a wakeup call," Suzanne said softly, squinting at him from beneath the hanging light. "Seeing Joanie, lying to her, was a wakeup call. I need help. I just want to get better. I don't care about anything you've done. I promise I won't say a word to anyone."

"Suzanne, Suzanne, you forget how well I know you." He put his elbows on the table, locked fingers, and stared into her eyes. "You saw the drug operation. You saw what happened to poor Timmy."

Suzanne looked down at the table.

"I know you're craving more oxy. Let me give you a decent bump and have you get a good night's sleep. Everything will be better in the morning."

The longing look on her pretty face was just like every other time. She would give in once presented with the pills. Not only would she give in, but her hands would be trembling violently as she rushed those pills to her lovely mouth.

Footsteps on the staircase.

"Okay, that's done." Mars entered the room holding a green duffle bag. He went straight for the bar, dropped the bag, and poured a glass of bourbon. He took a drink and sighed. "All Timmy's clothes, phone, pipe, ring, bracelet, belongings are in this bag, as instructed by Raymond G."

The doorbell rang.

Suzanne looked alertly toward the foyer.

Octavius looked at Mars, who scowled and looked at his watch.

"He couldn't be here yet," Mars said. "I'll see who it is." He set his drink down and headed toward the foyer.

"Stop!" Octavius said. "Stay put. Listen."

None of them moved a muscle. They listened intently.

People's footsteps and soft voices came from just beyond the front door.

Octavius was certain it was a SWAT team.

It's over.

Then singing began outside.

Joy to the World, the Lord is come!
Let earth - receive - her King
Let every heart - prepare Him room
And Heaven and nature sing
And Heaven and nature sing

And Heaven, and Heaven, and nature sing

Octavius dropped his head in relief.

Mars let out a sigh and a string of expletives.

"Carolers," Suzanne said in monotone, as if they were angels singing directly to her.

They continued singing, probably knowing people were inside because lights were on and Mars's car was in the driveway.

. . . While fields and floods, rocks, hills and plains
Repeat the sounding joy
Repeat the sounding joy
Repeat, repeat, the sounding joy

"Okay, enough already!" Mars said.

"Keep your cool, mayor," Octavius said.

When the voices finally stopped and the sound of footsteps tapered off into the night, Suzanne's head dropped to the table, as if her last hope had just burned out. Octavius guessed that, due to the current crucible she found herself in, Suzanne was reaching back to her Christian roots for some sort of hope or miracle.

Good luck with that.

"I'm starved," Mars said. He walked toward the kitchen.

"You know where the pantry is," Octavius said. "Have whatever you can find."

Mars opened the fridge. He pulled out the leftovers from the dinner Octavius had cooked for Joanie and Wayne. He found a plate and fork, and served himself a glob of noodles and shrimp.

The smell of spices filled the air.

"Your famous Thai?" Mars said, tossing his tie over his shoulder.

"That's right."

"Spicy!" Mars said with a mouthful.

Octavius was somewhat amazed at how quickly Mars seemed to have gotten over Timmy's demise. It made him wonder once again what other deviant behavior Mars had been involved with in the past.

"There's more in there that's not spicy," Octavius said.

Mars ignored him and continued to shovel in large forkfuls of the food.

"Where is this guy?" Octavius said, wanting to get Timmy out of there.

"He'll be here. He's coming from Jessup." Mars clinked his fork on the plate and wiped his mouth. "Can we talk—in private?" Mars glared at Octavius, then took his plate to the sink and turned on the water.

Octavius looked at Suzanne, who was staring at him with pleading eyes. He slid out of the booth with a grunt and went to the kitchen where Mars was drying his hands on a towel. Mars tossed the towel on the counter and walked to the far end of the kitchen, out of Suzanne's earshot. He squared his big shoulders with his back to Suzanne and looked up at Octavius.

"You know what I'm going to say," Mars said.

"I'm still figuring out what we're going to do with her."

"We?" Mars huffed. "There's no 'we' about it."

"Right. Okay. Well, you're just going to have to trust me," Octavius said.

"Look, we both want to weather this storm. I think we can do it, cleanly. I think we can get right back on track." He paused, then rubbed the back of his neck and winced as if in pain. "But Suzanne's a loose end that's going to unravel everything. We both know it. You agree, don't you?"

Octavius did not like being put in a spot where he had to trust another person so much. Yes, he'd had to trust Mars with knowledge of the drug operation, but now there had been a killing. That had changed everything. The confidence Octavius would need to put in Mars to keep that a secret was much, much more than he'd ever dared to put in another human being.

"We can have Raymond G take her," Mars whispered. "I'm telling you—this guy is a miracle worker. He's quiet, he's clean . . . After tonight, all our worries will be gone."

Hmm.

Perhaps Raymond G was the solution for Suzanne.

"What do you say?" Mars said.

Octavius glanced over at Suzanne.

She was gone.

30

Deetz thought about how lovely Joanie was as he watched her gracefully make her way back to their table from across the dark, romantically-lit dining room of The Mainstay restaurant.

He reached over and pulled her chair out for her. The music for "White Christmas" played softly in the background. "You didn't even get to the restroom, did you?" he said.

"No. I wanted to get back. Sorry I was gone so long." She sat, almost out of breath, and nudged her chair up to the table. She looked tense.

"You've got time. Go ahead," Wayne said.

"That was her, the mayor's wife." Joanie looked back over into the bar then leaned toward Wayne with a serious face. "Suzanne's still in Sedona."

"You're kidding me."

She shook her head. "She's at StoneSpell with Octavius right now. They're with the mayor and that other rich guy I read about online—the one they took the boat to in Charleston, Timmy Kondore."

"She knows for a fact Suzanne's here in town—for sure?"

Joanie nodded and cleared her throat. She looked nervous. Then her eyes widened and she smiled, acknowledging Dawson and a server who had arrived at the table with their entrees.

After Dawson made sure everything was satisfactory, Wayne

gave thanks for the food, they toasted, and took first bites. Wayne could tell from Joanie's posture and the creases in her forehead that she was upset to confirm that Suzanne had lied about leaving town.

"Everything's delicious," Joanie said.

But Wayne could tell she was shaken from the conversation with Candace.

"What else did she say? Lay it on me," Wayne said. "You're upset, I can tell."

"I don't want to spoil this evening." She blinked back her emotions.

"Honey, it's okay. My curiosity is killing me."

"Well, Candace is smashed, first of all, so she spoke *very* freely." Joanie took a sip of water. "She said there's an 'SOS at StoneSpell.' A man named Raymond G is on his way there and when this particular guy gets involved, 'it's never good.' The mayor called her while I was standing there and asked her for this guy's contact info, this Raymond G. She texted it to him." Joanie leaned back in her chair and shook her head, suppressing the emotion with a frown.

"Okay, okay, calm down," Wayne said. "Can you try to enjoy your dinner while we talk? Try to relax."

Joanie took a bite and spoke. "She said if I'm Suzanne's friend I need to tell her to get out of that house, right now." Joanie broke down, her shoulders wilted, her hands dropped on the table, still holding her fork and knife. "This has been a nightmare. I'm so sorry, Wayne. This is ruining a special night."

He covered one of her hands with his. "Don't worry, babe. It's okay. We're fine. We're fine, okay? We can call Suzanne now if you want to."

That really made Joanie cry, probably because she was relieved he was taking the Suzanne saga in stride.

"You've been looking forward to this so much." She sniffed and wiped her nose with her napkin.

"Well, just the fact she lied to you about leaving town, and now this? It's crazy. Call her and warn her, like the lady said. That's about all you can do."

It didn't take any more coaxing than that. Joanie brought her purse around from the back of her chair, found her phone, and punched in Suzanne's number.

Wayne reached over and took another bite of Joanie's ribs.

"Have all you want," she whispered while listening to Suzanne's phone ring.

After another ten seconds, Joanie pursed her lips, shook her head, and lowered the phone. "Voicemail. What else is new?" she said. "Here, try my potatoes; they're unreal."

Wayne knew Joanie so well. She was trying valiantly to continue their romantic evening, but with the news flash from Candace Maddox about the 'SOS at StoneSpell,' things had taken a definite and unavoidable shift.

"Maybe we should call the police," Joanie said.

Wayne closed his eyes briefly and told himself to be gentle. "Honey, based on what?" he said. "All you have is some conspiracy theory from a drunk woman."

Wayne took another bite of his entree. He could tell by the way Joanie picked at her food and forced a smile that she was not going to rest until she was sure Suzanne was okay.

"You're really something, you know that?" Wayne said.

"What do you mean?"

"You're worried about your friend, who completely dissed you, when you should be enjoying yourself. I wish I had your compassion."

"I'm worried for her, Wayne. If it was just her dodging me I could live with that, but you should have heard Candace. Something's going on over there *tonight*. I don't think she would have said any of it if she wasn't three sheets to the wind."

He sighed. Another enormous burst of laughter broke out from Candace and her pals in the bar. Joanie took a bite of her ribs and looked over that way. Wayne realized he could be her hero by cutting dinner short and stopping at StoneSpell on the way back to their place.

"What the heck," he said. "The lamb adobo wasn't all it was cracked up to be anyway." He wiped his mouth and set his big napkin on the table. "Let's blow this popsicle stand. Where's Dawson when you need him?"

"Honey, are you sure?" Joanie said, excitedly. "I'll make it up to you, I promise."

"Oh, I'll hold you to that." He spotted Dawson across the room and signaled for him to come over. "We'll have him box these up. You need to be thinking about what you're going to say when we knock on the door at StoneSpell. I can only imagine what you'll come up with."

"I don't care if I make a complete fool of myself. Who cares what any of them think?"

SUZANNE DASHED FOR THE STAIRS, flew down to the basement, and stopped five feet from Timmy Kondore's stark white corpse and the dark burgundy puddle of blood beneath him. She heard Octavius yell. Heart pounding, she looked both ways and took off down a long hallway, hoping to find a way outside.

She heard footsteps descending the stairs as she ran.
She gambled on the door at the end of the hall.
She ran for it as fast as she could.
It opened.
Thank God.
The room was pitch black.
She went in.
Concrete floor. Cold air.
Likely an unfinished portion of the basement.
There had to be a door leading outside.
But she couldn't see and had no phone, no light.
There had to be a light switch.
She closed the door.
She patted the wall, which was not a wall but slats of wood.
One of the men yelled her name in anger.

A protruding splinter of wood stuck her hand. She pulled away in pain and continued patting the wood with trembling hands.

There was no switch. It was probably one of those bare bulbs that hung in the center of the room with a string hanging from it.

She covered her eyes so she could adjust more quickly to the dark.

Whoever was after her was opening each door along the hallway in search of her.

In the distance some twenty feet across the black room, she spotted a slight reflection—in a window. She walked carefully toward it, not wanting to bash into anything. She got to it, turned the latch on the sill, and pushed to open with both hands. It was stuck. She could barely breath she was so nervous. The one hand pulsed in pain. She bashed the top of the sill with her good hand and the window budged. She pushed it up as high as it would go and stuck a leg out. She sat on the ledge, scrunched over to get her upper body through the opening, and brought her other leg through to the outside.

Her feet hit gravel.

She looked all around to get her bearings. It was freezing and she could see her breath. She was at the far end of StoneSpell and the street light was coming from around to the right. She began to hurry that way but it was going to be difficult to see the ground in front of her.

A bright light lit up the unfinished basement from which she'd just escaped and she saw the mayor heading for the window in his white dress shirt and suspenders. She could see now there was a door right next to the window she'd jumped out. If she hadn't been so scared it would have been funny.

She feared Octavius would be at the front of the house waiting for her.

She heard a latch and saw Mars coming out the basement door with his phone lit up to serve as a flashlight.

She turned and ran in the direction of the street, but she stumbled because it was so dark and the ground was uneven.

Then she saw her own shadow cast by the light from Mars's phone, and she heard him panting, coming from behind, cursing.

If she could get to a neighbor's house she would barge in and call the police.

She just needed to get to the street so she could run on level ground.

"You shouldn't have done that, Suzanne."

It was Octavius's voice, out of breath, coming from her right, followed by a piercing pop, loud clicking and static electricity, and fissures of light—from a taser.

Her body arched.

Her back locked up as every muscle head to toe contracted and pulsed violently.

She heard herself scream. The pain was widespread and unspeakable—and felt as if it would never end.

When it finally did, she dropped to the ground.

Alive.

But for how long?

31

THE CAR WAS quiet on the way to StoneSpell and Joanie hoped Wayne wasn't too upset they'd left dinner early.

"Thanks for doing this." She reached for his right hand while he drove. "And thanks for a lovely evening."

"You're welcome." Wayne squeezed her hand. "I'm tired. Looking forward to that luxurious bed."

If he was upset, he was hiding it well. While he seemed to be taking the 'SOS' at StoneSpell lightly, Joanie was wired. She just had a feeling they were about to walk into the middle of something bizarre; the whole experience with Suzanne had been so strange. She shivered and pulled the collar of the fleece jacket tighter around her neck.

"Want more heat?" Wayne said.

"I'm good, thanks. I'm nervous."

"Have you thought about what you're going to say when we go to the door?"

"I was thinking I could just say I talked to Suzanne's mom today and she thought Suzanne was still in Sedona," Joanie said. "I can say I thought she may've changed plans and I couldn't reach her by phone. We had dinner nearby and decided to stop in."

"That'll work."

"I wish you had your gun and badge."

Wayne looked over and stared at her for a few seconds then looked back at the road. "Wow, you're expecting the worst."

"I don't have a good feeling."

"Hmm. Maybe I should go to the door alone," Wayne said. "I don't mind."

"Let's see how it feels when we get there."

"How far?" Wayne jokingly squinted at the GPS. "The numbers are so small."

Joanie laughed and examined the GPS. "ETA eight minutes, old man."

OCTAVIUS WAS ON A MISSION NOW.

It was up to him to bring order to the chaos the others had created.

After getting Suzanne back inside StoneSpell, he had ordered Mars to watch her at gunpoint in the living room while he prepared a long overdue drug cocktail for her.

"What's the word from your guy?" Octavius said as he approached Mars and Suzanne holding a tall glass of lime seltzer water, laced with enough China White powder to sedate a horse.

"I'm not expecting to hear any more from him," Mars said flatly. "He said he'd be here, he'll be here. Relax."

Octavius shook his head at Mars, disgusted. Then he just stood there over Suzanne with the drink. She was seated in a straight-back chair Mars had brought in from the dining room. Mars was seated in a similar chair next to her tossing his pea shooter back and forth in his fat hands.

Looking at the glass Suzanne shook her head ever so slightly, but Octavius knew that deep down she wanted it desperately.

"Take a walk, Mars," Octavius said.

Mars glared up at him. After a good fifteen seconds he finally heaved himself out of the chair and crossed to the bar.

Octavius sat with a huff next to Suzanne.

"You're not who I thought you were," she said.

He smirked.

Her head dropped. "I can't believe how stupid I've been."

"Drink this." He held the glass out to her.

She looked at it, then at him. "I don't want that."

He sighed and his shoulders slumped.

"Look, I get it," he said. "You want to get clean. That's fine. But now's not the time. And you need professional help to do it. You can't just stop in a day."

"You want me to drink it because you need me to go away."

"For a little while, yes. This is going to set you free. Once we get this situation behind us, then you and I will talk about our future."

"We?" She spewed the word out as if she'd just tasted gasoline. "*We* have no future, you loser. What are you going to do, throw me into your dungeon with those other women? You just killed a man!"

Octavius's nostrils flared. He glanced across the vast room at Mars who appeared to be immersed on his phone.

Octavius told himself to remain calm. He sighed and leaned toward Suzanne. In his most alluring tone he said, "Just drink. You're almost there. Almost to that happy place. Come on, Suzanne, you want this."

She looked longingly at the glass as if it was the holy grail.

Then in a flash she smacked it out of his hand.

The glass shattered on the floor at his feet.

Octavius slapped her face so hard it hurt his hand. Her head whipped to one side and her cheek was instantly dark red.

But she didn't make a sound. Just put a hand on the welt and dropped her head to her chest.

Mars stood there staring at them with a fresh drink in one hand and his phone in the other.

Octavius stood nonchalantly and headed for the kitchen. "Get ready to hold her down, Mars. We're going to have to do this the hard way."

32

Deetz pulled the SUV into the circular driveway at StoneSpell and his headlights lit up an expensive dark gray Audi sedan. Its Arizona license plate read: Mayor MM.

"See the plates?" Joanie said.

"Mars Maddox," Wayne said.

"Candace is batting a thousand so far," Joanie said. "Suzanne's got to be in there."

Deetz eased the car to a stop, shut it off, and looked over at Joanie. She peered at the sleek house, which was much darker than the night they'd come for dinner. There was a soft light on inside, perhaps from the living room.

"I don't see the Benz," Wayne said. "Or Suzanne's car."

"Could be in the garage. I'm nervous as all get-out."

All the garage doors were closed.

"I guess the mysterious Raymond G isn't here yet, unless he rode with the mayor," Wayne said.

They sat in silence for a few moments just watching for any movement inside. The interior of the car smelled like the food in the to-go boxes. The night was cold and quiet.

"You want to try calling her once more before we do this?" Wayne said.

"I guess." Joanie turned on her phone, punched Suzanne's number, and listened as it rang.

SUZANNE HAD FOUGHT with everything in her. She'd scratched Mars's face and kicked Octavius good in the kneecap. In the end, the two men had pinned her down and forced her to drink as much of the drug-laced beverage as they could. She'd kept her mouth shut as much as she could, and about half of it had spilled down the side of her face.

In a way, Suzanne had wanted it. After all, pain killers had been the sole thing she'd lived for over the past year or more. But having seen Octavius shoot and kill the Kondore man in cold blood terrorized and awakened Suzanne. She just wanted to be sober. She wanted to change. She wanted God in her life again.

She knew if she took any more drugs she would be easy prey for Octavius and Mars—but that's exactly what had happened. After they forced her to drink, Octavius roughly escorted her downstairs. She tried to fight him, but he easily overpowered her. When he lifted the staircase, she ran, but he caught up to her in four giant steps and bashed her to the ground, hurting her right shoulder badly and cutting her lip.

After unlocking the heavy bronze metal door behind the raised steps, he threw her to the floor with a cuss and slammed it shut.

She was light-headed and felt as if she'd been given a sleeping tranquilizer. She remained on the floor in the dark room for what must have been ten to thirty minutes, dozing in and out of consciousness. When she awoke and her eyes adjusted to the dark, she made out the shape of two beds—one on each side of the room.

She'd been there before.

OCTAVIUS RETURNED from his master bathroom limping toward the bar, and handed Mars the brown bottle of hydrogen peroxide and a handful of cotton balls to clean the two-inch scratch on his face.

Mars set the stuff on the bar next to his gun without a word, threw back the last of his drink, and began to pour another.

"You better go easy on that," Octavius said. "We've got work to do tonight."

"*We're* not doing anything. This guy will handle it. That's why we're paying him the big bucks," Mars said.

"How much?"

"Depends how many people he takes out of here." Mars stopped suddenly, cussed, and looked around the vast living room. He probably just remembered Octavius had cameras everywhere and that he had just been recorded.

Mars took a gulp of the bourbon he'd just poured, as if to infuriate Octavius, then began dowsing cotton balls with hydrogen peroxide. He looked in the mirror wall at the bar and dabbed at the scratch on his face. "She got me good." He winced and cursed as he cleaned it.

"Feels like she broke my kneecap." Octavius laughed, but Mars didn't.

"How much will this guy charge for just Timmy?" Octavius reached for his pipe and tobacco.

"Does it really matter, Octavius? It's a necessity. Besides, with Timmy out of the picture." He stopped again, chewed his bottom lip, and shook his head.

"I'm trying to gauge how much it would be if he took Suzanne, too."

"Again, necessity. Who cares? You're making bank," Mars said, scrolling through his phone. "I'll talk to him when he gets here. You stay out of it. You don't need to say one word to him."

"Are we talking a hundred grand? Five hundred grand?" Octavius lit up his pipe and toked on it.

Mars looked up from his phone and locked eyes with Octavius.

"Full disclosure," Octavius said. "I have two other women down there."

"I figured," Mars said.

"What if I want him to take them, too? Start over with a clean slate."

"Is that what you want me to ask him?"

Octavius paused and smoked. "I'd like to get a price for that, yes."

Mars mumbled exasperatedly and shook his head. "This isn't

Walmart. So, if he doesn't give you the buy-three-get-one-free deal you're not gonna do it? Forget about the money, man. Think about the future."

"Okay then, I want you to arrange it with him. Try to get the best deal you can, of course."

"He wasn't expecting this. Not even close. I told him about one —not four. We'll see what he says. By the way, you need to turn off all your slimy little cameras."

"A little late for that now, don't you think?" With pipe in mouth, Octavius pulled his gun from the back of his waistband and shoved it in the front of his belt. "Carrying one of these isn't as easy as they make it look on TV."

The doorbell rang.

The two men looked at each other.

"That's him." Mars tucked the gun in the back of his suit pants.

"It's about time."

"Go turn the cameras off," Mars said. "I'll get the door."

"Dab that cut again. It's still bleeding." Octavius headed toward the basement steps. He had no intention of turning the cameras off, but he would play along.

33

Joanie dropped back a few feet as Wayne stepped up to the main entrance of StoneSpell, rang the lighted doorbell again, and backed away from the massive doors. He had many years of experience standing at ominous thresholds, awaiting the answer of hardened criminals, and it showed in his even demeanor. Joanie, on the other hand, shivered with edginess as they waited and occasionally glanced at each other.

"It's okay," Wayne whispered. "It'll be fine. God's got this."

Joanie took solace in the reminder momentarily, but her uneasiness was overwhelming. The night before when they'd come to StoneSpell for dinner, the front entrance and entire house were festively lit and music played throughout. Now, it was dark, windy, and hauntingly quiet. Joanie hoped this wasn't a foreshadowing of the things about to happen.

Heavy footsteps approached the doors from inside the house and one of the doors lurched open. Mayor Marsden Maddox stood there frozen with his mouth gaping open. He had a glass of bourbon in one hand and a glistening cut on his face that needed stitches or at least butterfly bandages.

His face instantly confirmed Joanie's suspicion that there was trouble inside StoneSpell.

Mars closed the door until it was open just the width of his wide head. "Can I help you?"

"Hi, yes," Joanie said, flustered. "Is Octavius home?"

"No. Sorry, he's out. I'm a friend." Mars closed the door even further and turned the injured half of his face away from them. "What's this about?"

"We're friends also—Joanie and Wayne Deetz," said Joanie. "Really, long-time friends of his girlfriend, Suzanne."

"Okay. I'll tell them you stopped." Mars began to shut the door.

"Aren't you Mayor Maddox?" Joanie said, hoping to play on the vanity she'd witnessed on his website.

The door stopped closing. He peered out through a four-inch opening. He looked past them to his car, probably thinking of his license plate. "I am. It's good to meet you. Sorry, I've got to run." He forced a smile. "I'm the chef tonight."

Again, the door began to shut.

"Is Suzanne inside?" Wayne said. "We're having a hard time reaching her."

The door was open just two inches and Mars was no longer looking out. He simply said, "Nope. She and Octavius have gone to the airport . . . to pick up my wife. She's flying in tonight. I'm in charge of dinner. Don't want it to burn. Bye now."

The door closed with a thud, and locked. Mars's footsteps retreated into the house.

The alcohol from his breath hung in the air.

Joanie looked at Wayne and started to freak out.

Wayne put a finger to his lips. "Let's go to the car. We'll talk there." He took her arm and walked her down the large stone steps toward the SUV.

They got in and Wayne turned on the car.

"He lied! He said Candace is flying in. We just saw her!" Joanie's heart was beating so fast it felt like it was going to explode. "That's a fresh cut on his face! They're in there, Wayne. He's hiding something! Why would he answer the door?"

Wayne leaned back against the headrest, squeezed his nose, and rubbed his chin.

"You agree something's wrong, right?" she said.

"Yeah. I'm trying to figure out what to do."

Joanie knew he would know the best thing to do so she made

herself shut up, but her insides pulsed with fury and a profound sense of urgency.

Wayne reached for his phone, tapped at the screen, and put it to his ear. "I'm calling the police."

Joanie nodded and closed her eyes and prayed silently.

Wayne leaned up to the dash, squinted at the glowing GPS screen, and spoke to the 911 operator after she asked him to explain his emergency. "I'm at seven-two-zero Canyon Trail in Sedona. My name is Wayne Deetz, thirty-five year investigator with the Portland Police Department in Portland, Oregon. I have reason to believe a crime is happening right now at this address. It's a residence. Owner's name is Octavius Hunt."

Wayne covered the mic and told Joanie he was going to do what he needed to do to get an officer out there. She nodded anxiously in agreement.

"I believe a woman is being held against her will inside the house. Her name is Suzanne Bartholomew," Wayne said. "She lives in Red Rock City at the Adobe Village Apartments."

Again, the operator spoke. Joanie couldn't hear what she was saying.

Wayne answered, "She told my wife and me that she was getting on an airplane to go to Bend, Oregon, this morning but that never happened. We spoke to her mom and confirmed that. We have reason to believe she's in the house, possibly being held under duress. Jessup Mayor Marsden Maddox is also in the house with a fresh cut on his face. We were just at the door talking to him. He wanted to get rid of us. He lied to us about Suzanne's whereabout and also about his wife's whereabouts."

Wayne eyed Joanie while the operator spoke in his ear.

"He would not let us in the house. We also know a man named Raymond G is due to arrive here soon and we understand he's trouble, as in likely has a long rap sheet. Please, if you can send a car out and just have your officers go inside the house for a walkthrough—that's what's needed. I don't have a gun or badge with me, besides, I'm out of my jurisdiction. I'm not aware of Arizona's rules on territorial jurisdiction, but I wouldn't go in the house anyway right now without a weapon."

Wayne raised his eyebrows and threw his free hand up as if to say, "I'm not sure if this will work."

Please God. Please God. Please God.

After a long delay, Wayne perked up in his seat. "Yes, I will wait here!" He nodded and smiled excitedly and gave a thumbs up. "I'll park up along the street. I'm in a red SUV. I can brief your officers . . . It's Deetz, Wayne Deetz. Portland PD." He spelled his last name for the operator, then waited as she spoke.

"Thank you *very* much," Wayne said.

He ended the call, squeezed Joanie's hand, put the car in drive, and began to head out of the circular driveway. "There's a car within ten minutes of us. Now we wait."

34

WITH HIS BACK to the wall just around the corner from the foyer, Octavius had heard Mars's entire conversation with Wayne and Joanie Deetz—and he was livid.

When Mars came back into the living room with a sloppy gait due to too much alcohol, Octavius was waiting for him. He threw his hands up in disgust.

"How could they possibly know who you are?" Octavius said.

"How should I know?" Mars yelled right back. "Who are they, anyway, and what are they doing here at this time of night?"

"That guy's a cop!" Octavius yelled.

"What?" Mars's bloodshot eyes were huge.

"From Portland. They're friends of Suzanne's. On vacation."

Mars turned around and headed back to the foyer. His revolver was stuffed in the back of his belt. Octavius assumed he was making sure the Deetzes had left.

"Are they gone?" Octavius called.

Mars was silent.

Octavius quick-stepped into the front room and peaked out one of the windows.

The Deetzes were still sitting in their car.

"They saw your cut," Octavius said.

"How was I supposed to know you were going to have people

show up now? We both thought it was Raymond G. Get off my back. That's on you that they showed up."

"Why on earth did you lie about Candace flying in and all that? What was that? It made no sense. That could come back to haunt us later. It will!"

"I had to explain why I was answering *your* door." Mars slurred his words.

What a mess.

Finally, the Deetz's car rolled out of the driveway.

Octavius let out a sigh of relief.

The two men went back into the living room.

"If Suzanne disappears now the cops are marching straight to you." Octavius said.

"And not you?" Mars yelled, then laughed. "This is *your* house, you idiot! You think you're so above everyone, so suave and untouchable, yet here we are in the middle of a crap storm you created." Mars was so animated that he ran out of breath. "You're not going to be able to charm your way out of this one!"

"Where the heck is your guy?" Octavius yelled. "He's late!"

"He'll be here."

"Timmy's first on the list. He's the priority." Octavius tried to calm himself down. He was feeling way too out of control. "Maybe we ought to hold off on Suzanne and the others. Get rid of Timmy, get this place clean, let some time pass."

Mars turned, walked to the bar, and got a new glass.

"You're not drinking anymore—not till Raymond's come and gone," Octavius said.

Mars turned and faced Octavius. They glared at each other for a long time. "I've got a news flash for you, my friend. After tonight, we're done," Mars said, then turned his back on Octavius and sloshed more whiskey into the glass.

"What's that supposed to mean?" Octavius said.

"I can't afford to be associated with you." Mars glanced at Octavius's reflection in the mirror above the bar. "We're shutting down the drug operation."

"We are not doing any such thing," Octavius yelled. "You're drunk!"

Mars turned to face him. "Maybe so. Maybe that's what I needed in order to be able to tell you. It's over. This has been brewing for a long time. Suzanne's a strung-out addict. She's blabbing—"

"We're not ending the operation!" Octavius ripped the heavy black gun from his belt. He didn't point it at Mars but waved it as he spoke. "If you want out, I'll buy you out."

Mars shook his head slowly. "You're a detriment. Three women in some dungeon in your basement? Killing Timmy? You're obviously going to get caught—and I'm not going to be around when you do. Put that gun away. It's not your style."

Octavius blinked back his rage and manufactured a rather psychotic laugh. There was no way the drug operation could stop. He clinked the gun down on the table at the booth and put his hands out as a peace sign to Mars.

"Okay Mars, let's not make any rash decisions tonight that we're going to regret," Octavius said. "We can talk about this tomorrow after we've both had some rest."

Mars drank.

"Okay?" Octavius said. "Can we agree to that?"

Octavius was barely breathing. This was a blip on the screen that he hadn't seen coming.

Mars looked down at his drink and said nothing.

The large room fell silent.

Octavius grew more desperate by the second. He needed the partnership with Mars to continue, but the longer he looked at the man, the more convinced he became that Mars had made up his mind to sever any dealings with Octavius. The despairing feeling took Octavius right back to his boyhood and reminded him of how Father Pat had stolen something from him—his very innocence. It had left him broken and scarred.

And now Marsden Maddox—leaning against the bar nonchalantly, thumbing through his big phone like some prima donna celebrity—was about to attempt to steal the very thing Octavius had built his life upon.

Did Mars really believe Octavius would fold that easily?
Narcissistic fool.
Octavius closed his eyes and calmed himself.
He breathed deeply, mindfully.
One thing at a time.

Raymond G would fix the Timmy situation.

Then Mars would drive Octavius back to his car at DoughWorx.

Mars would then commit suicide in his own car, with his own gun, right in the parking lot of DoughWorx—the ideal location for the distraught mayor to end it all. Before Octavius staged the tragedy, he would attempt to force Mars to write a brief goodbye note to Candace and the kids. Even just a few words would do the trick.

Octavius would then drive his own car back to StoneSpell, give the girls downstairs another round of meds, have a nightcap, and proceed to sleep like a baby.

Except for Wayne and Joanie Deetz.

They would keep him awake.

Because they'd been there that night. They'd seen the mayor with a gash on his face and a drink in his hand making up lies about Candace flying in from who knew where?

"I just texted Raymond G," Mars said. "He's seven minutes out."

35

Suzanne was dizzy and the pitch-black room wasn't helping her equilibrium. Normally in this condition she would have curled up and gone to sleep, but every fiber in her being urged her to stay awake, to prepare for a fight.

"Who are you?" came a female voice from the far left side of the room.

Suzanne paused, trying to make sure she heard what she'd heard.

"Hello?" came the voice again.

"Suzanne . . . Who are you?"

"Janine."

"Janine, where are the lights?" Suzanne said. "Can you turn a lamp on?"

"He keeps it like this. No lights. No windows. Get used to it."

Suzanne was still on the floor. The only light came from a dull turquoise nightlight plugged into the wall at a crooked angle some thirty feet across the room.

"How long have you been here?" Suzanne said.

"No idea. Years."

Years?

Suzanne felt as if she'd been punched in the gut. Octavius was a demon. And he'd had his way with her for more than a year. It sickened her.

"Years?" Suzanne whispered.

"I'm surprised you didn't hear about it in the news. At least, I assumed it would have made national headlines. Maybe it happens so much now, it didn't."

"Wait!" Suzanne's stomach tanked. "Are you from Florida? What's your last name?"

"Sharp. Yeah. Flagler Beach."

"I do remember! Your brother was on TV several times. He posted a reward. He fought like crazy to find you."

"Oh, I'm sure Randy raised Cain." Janine chuckled.

As Suzanne remembered that a mysterious man had been questioned extensively in the disappearance of Janine Sharp, she clapped a hand over her mouth and forced herself not to throw up.

Octavius.

He took her.

The room was silent and Suzanne's mind was blown.

Janine called across the room in a loud whisper, "Delia . . . Delia, you awake?"

There was no answer.

"Best we can figure Delia got here about a year after me," Janine said. "She remembers hearing about my disappearance, vaguely. Octavius let things cool down for a year, then he started stalking her."

There was a long pause. Suzanne waited in the dark for more, fighting a heavy grogginess.

"She and her husband had a framing business in Jessup." Janine's voice was weak, and she spoke in monotone. "Octavius started using them to custom frame his paintings; gave them a ton of business, paid big bucks, was overly particular. He came on strong to Delia. Her husband knew, but he and Delia kind of joked about it. Octavius has a thing for older women. Delia and Patrick have two kids nineteen and twenty-one; she's like forty-five."

Janine paused then called across the room again. "Delia. Delia . . ."

Delia didn't make a sound.

Janine fell back to her pillow and sighed, as if the story was taking a lot out of her.

"One night when Patrick was in Las Vegas at a business convention, Octavius asked to meet her for coffee to discuss business," Janine said softly. "He drugged her, put something in her drink while she was in the restroom. She didn't realize it at the time because—who does that? He got her alone, tied her up, and gave her a shot of something that made her really high. Then he made her write a note that she was leaving Patrick and that no one should look for her. She was leaving the country . . . I'm too tired. She can tell you the rest."

Suzanne heard the top from a plastic jug open, then heard Janine gulping.

"So . . . he forces you to stay here?" Suzanne realized it sounded stupid right after she'd said it, but she was feeling nauseous and weird and was just trying to stay awake and keep the conversation going.

"Only time we leave is to go to his so-called Chamber," Janine said. She drank more. The plastic bottle made denting sounds as if it was almost empty. She cussed. "We get a gallon of water a day, some bread, a TV dinner once or twice a week. Plus the drugs. All kinds of drugs—uppers, downers, painkillers, sleepers. A lot of times he sedates us and we're out for days. I can tell I'm due. He'll be coming soon."

"Have you ever tried to refuse?"

Janine laughed. "At first. So did Delia. But it was no use. He had us. When we realized there was no getting out, we gave in."

Suzanne understood. She, too, had ended up simply going along with Octavius's hypnotic regimen of drugs.

"Why are you here?" Janine said. "What's going on? I thought I heard a commotion."

Suzanne crawled closer to Janine's bed. "Octavius killed a man out there. I don't know what's going to happen. He's scrambling to clean up after himself. He may keep me in here, or he may try to get rid of me."

Janine grunted and moved around in her bed, trying to get comfortable. "There's another bed at the far end of the room, near the nightlight. You were here before . . . weren't you?"

"Yeah, but he had me so lit I don't remember," Suzanne said. "Is there anything in this room we can use for a weapon? Anything at all?"

"Don't bother, okay?" Janine rolled over and sighed. "The only possible thing is the metal bedframes. We took one apart, but the pieces are too long and heavy, too awkward. I've got to sleep."

Suzanne sat there in the dark another moment. She felt her swollen lip. Then she got to her knees and stood. But the room spun.

She dropped back to her knees.

She crawled toward the nightlight at the far end of the room and saw the silhouette of the twin bed. Her shoulder was killing her. She put her hands out on the bed and felt the cool blanket. She hoisted herself up and sprawled out on her stomach. There was no pillow; it didn't matter. She put one foot onto the floor to stop the spinning. She wasn't going to be able to stay awake much longer.

Jesus . . . rescue us.

36

Deetz had parked the SUV about fifty yards down the street from StoneSpell because he didn't want anyone inside the house to be able to see that they were still there. He and Joanie sat inside the toasty car with the engine idling. The street was quiet and mostly dark, except for the white neon glow of a streetlight that shown from down the street behind them. Only one car had passed since they'd parked.

"I'm so nervous," Joanie said.

Wayne reached over and squeezed the back of her neck.

"Oh my gosh, your hand is freezing," she said.

He pulled it away.

"No, it's okay. It feels good. I'm hot anyway." She turned down the heat. She couldn't sit still.

"Don't be nervous," Deetz said. "The police are on the way. They'll handle it—whatever's going on."

He decided to lighten the mood.

"You know what I'm going to do when we get back to the house?" he said.

"Uh-uh."

"I'm going to get my pj's on, heat up my leftovers, and have a little feast while I read my book. Delightful."

Silence.

"Where is this cop?" Joanie said.

Wayne noticed headlights coming toward them way in the distance.

"This might be them," he said.

They both watched in silence as the headlights approached at a good clip, then slowed about four houses down from StoneSpell.

"That's him. He's looking for the address," Joanie said.

But Wayne didn't think it was a squad car.

"Hold up," he said. "Scrunch down and be still."

They both dropped low in their seats and watched.

The white van with no windows slowly turned into the circular drive at StoneSpell. Its engine rumbled loudly. Green and blue lettering on the side of the truck read: Blake's Carpet Cleaning - Residential & Commercial," along with a phone number.

"Raymond G?" Joanie whispered.

"Maybe." Wayne looked all around for the Sedona Police car that should be coming. Then he watched as the large van squeezed past the Mayor's Audi, pulled right up next to the front doors of Stone-Spell, stopped and idled there with clouds of exhaust chugging out into the cold night.

The engine roared momentarily, then shut off. The driver's window was tinted. Nothing happened for what felt like a whole minute. Then the driver's door pushed open.

A man jumped out. He was white, not tall. Solid build with a large hard belly. He wore jeans, shiny brown cowboy boots, and a maroon short-sleeved polo shirt. He had a red face, flowing white hair, black-rimmed glasses, and a massive gold watch.

He walked along the side of the truck, his breath visible in the night air, and opened one of the two back doors. He reached in, pulled out a huge black leather satchel, threw it over a shoulder, and slammed the door. From there he ambled up the front steps and knocked on the door. It opened quickly and he disappeared inside.

"What is going on?" Joanie's voice broke the silence.

Wayne shook his head. "Could be anything. Could be good, could be bad." But he was leaning toward the latter. After all, the mayor answered Octavius's door with a fresh cut on his face. Suzanne had lied about leaving Sedona. Candace said all of them were together at StoneSpell, where there was a mysterious 'SOS.'

And a man named Raymond G had just shown up after 9 p.m. with what looked like a heavy bag of tools.

"Here comes someone." Joanie pointed forward at approaching headlights. "Maybe this is the police."

"Hope so."

The car drove slowly. As it approached the stone column mailbox at StoneSpell, Wayne could see a large black ram bar on front of the SUV and turret lights across the roof.

"That's them." Wayne flashed his headlights several times.

The black Ford Explorer accelerated past the driveway at Stone-Spell, came toward Wayne and Joanie's car, and flicked on its bright lights—lighting up the interior of Deetz's car. The headlights then flicked back to low beam and the car pulled up beside them. Both drivers put their windows down.

"Wayne Deetz?" asked the black female officer.

"Yes. Thanks for coming."

"I'm Officer Quincy." She was riding alone. She looked about thirty. Brown hair pulled back tight below a dark navy police ski cap. "You're police?" she said.

He nodded. "Portland PD. Thirty-five years. I don't have my badge. We're actually on vacation."

She asked for his driver's license and he gave it to her.

As she looked at it she said, "Can you explain why you called us?"

Wayne quickly went through the whole story. It took about two minutes. When he was finished, Officer Quincy handed Wayne his license.

"I'm going to pull in and run the plates on the cars in the driveway," Quincy said. "I'll likely go to the door and take a walk-through, make sure everything's okay. You guys can take off. No need for you to stick around."

Joanie started to object, but Wayne spoke over her. "If it's okay with you, we'll wait here. Suzanne's a close friend. We just want to make sure she's okay."

Officer Quincy stared at them for a second. She had a cleft lip that was barely noticeable, a small mouth with full lips, and a slender face. "I don't want you coming on the premises. You said you're not armed, correct?"

"Correct."

She nodded. "I'll stop here on my way out to let you know what's going on."

Quincy's window went up as she pulled away.

She turned the Explorer around in a driveway behind them and pulled back around them, then up a ways and into the driveway at StoneSpell. The words Sedona Police were painted in blue, white, and brown lettering on the side of the car. She eased to a stop behind the van and the Audi.

37

Octavius watched as Mars nodded a greeting to Raymond G, closed the front door, and escorted him into the foyer without a word. There, the bulky white-haired man held up a thick hand, set his big leather bag on the floor with a clink, leaned his back against a wall, bent over with a grunt, and slipped light-blue hygienic shoe coverings over each of his glossy cowboy boots. A half-inch-thick gold necklace shimmered and dangled around his neck as he did so.

Raymond G then stood, hoisted the bag over his shoulder, and followed Mars into the living room with kind of an easygoing, penguin-type gait. His posture was ramrod straight.

"Do you need anything at all from us?" Mars said.

Raymond G glanced at Octavius, shook his head no, and did a slow three-hundred-sixty-degree scan of the downstairs. Octavius wondered if, with his seemingly trained eye, the man might spot any of his hidden cameras.

"Hello," Octavius nodded at Raymond G. "Thank you for coming."

Mars shot Octavius a sour look and rolled his eyes.

Raymond G acted as if he hadn't heard him. The man's face was bright red with a smattering of white beard stubble and tiny purple veins across his nose and cheeks—much like that of a heavy drinker. He wasn't wearing a coat and the shoulders of his short-sleeved shirt were dusted in white flecks of dandruff. His nose seemed to be running and he continually sniffed and wiped it with the back of his thick wrists.

"You probably want to get to it." Mars clapped his hands. "Come this way."

Octavius stood in the living room and watched as Mars led the man to the basement staircase. Raymond G began snapping on black plastic surgical gloves as he descended.

Octavius remembered his gun on the table and crossed to get it; he stuffed it into the front of his pants. His leg was still smarting from where Suzanne had booted him. He went and got his pipe, loaded it with tobacco, and fired it up.

Mars returned from the basement. "He's all business—doesn't want me down there."

Octavius sat down and puffed on his pipe, not wanting to hear any more from Mars.

"Timmy's old man's going to be on a witch-hunt when he realizes his only son is missing," Mars said. "It ain't going to be pretty."

"But he's not going to find anything because your guy in the basement is so good, right?" Octavius said.

"Maybe you ought to consider starting over somewhere else." Mars opened the refrigerator and bent down to look inside. "Take Suzanne with you. Get her some help. Get a fresh start."

Octavius's eyes burned lasers into Mars, who wasn't looking at him.

"Let the other women go—whoever they are," Mars said.

"I'm just developing a name in Jessup, Mars. I can't leave now," Octavius said. "Besides, our business is booming. This is no time to tap the brakes. This whole thing is a blip on the screen."

The doorbell rang.

Mars dropped a plastic container of food and cussed.

Octavius shot to his feet.

"You get it," Mars said.

Octavius stared at him, thinking, thinking, thinking.

Mars's car's out front. It's obvious he's here. I can't hide that . . .
Who can it be? Candace?
The Deetzes again? Maybe that old cop suspects something . . .

It rang again.

"Go!" Mars hissed.

Octavius set his pipe in the ashtray. On his way to the door, he took out his gun and jammed it into the back of his pants and pulled his shirt over it. He figured he needed to have it with him. Things had gotten way out of control and he felt his world of make-believe was caving in on him.

Fingers snapped loudly several times. It was Raymond G. "Who is that?" he said out of breath, standing there peeling off the black rubber gloves.

"Don't know," Octavius said.

"Get rid of them—*fast*," Raymond G said.

"Duh. Ya think? Go back to what you were doing." Octavius continued toward the foyer, sick of all the flack he was getting from Mars and his over-the-hill hitman cleanup crew.

In the foyer, Octavius checked himself in the mirror, brushed his shoulders, forced a smile, and crossed to the front door. Mars and Raymond G had quietly made their way into the formal dining room just around the corner.

Octavius pulled the door open and there stood a female cop in her dark navy Sedona Police Department uniform, coat and hat, gloved hands on her waist.

"Octavius Hunt?" she said.

"Yes . . . good evening, officer," Octavius said as brightly as he could. "What can I do for you?"

"I'm Officer Quincy with the Sedona Police Department. I want to ask you about the van in your driveway." She nodded back toward it. "Is the owner in the house with you?"

Octavius could only imagine what Raymond G must be thinking.

"Uh . . . no. Actually, that was left here by someone," Octavius said. "A friend of a friend. I think he's due to pick it up in a day or two. What's going on, officer?"

"Do you mind if I step inside?" Quincy said.

"Well . . . I do have company at the moment."

"It won't take long." Quincy gently nudged her way into the foyer, looking all around as she did. "Beautiful home."

"Thank you." Octavius stepped to the front door, glanced out at

Quincy's black police SUV in the driveway, breathed a sigh of relief that there were no other cops in sight, and closed the door.

"Is Mayor Maddox here? I noticed his car out there." Quincy looked Octavius directly in the eyes. She was quite tall and had piercing brown eyes, the whites of which were clear and white as snow.

"He is, as a matter of fact."

"Can you get him, please? I don't want to have to ask the same questions twice." Quincy adjusted her stance and looked around confidently.

Mars came around the corner as if on cue.

"Well, well, well—who do we have here? Sedona's finest?" Mars said.

Quincy gave a brief smile but zeroed in on the gash on Mars's face.

"Mayor, hello. I'm Officer Quincy. I believe we met at the Jessup Fair. I was one of the officers who escorted you the evening you were master of ceremonies."

"Well, I certainly do remember, Quincy. What brings you to StoneSpell?"

"StoneSpell?" Quincy flicked her eyes back and forth in question.

Octavius chuckled nervously. "It's the name of the residence."

Quincy nodded with a blank look on her face. "Mayor, do you know who owns the van parked outside?"

Mars shook his head with a dumb look on his face, then looked questioningly at Octavius. "Didn't you say it was a friend of yours?"

"Yeah, I explained." Octavius was afraid his annoyance with Quincy was rising to the surface.

"The plates on it are bogus," Quincy said. "There's also no business by that name in the area. I'll need to get the contact info of the owner from you."

"Of course," Octavius said, and just stood there.

This is going sideways!

"How'd you get the cut on your face, mayor? That's a good one," Quincy said.

"Oh . . . ha." Mars laughed nervously, rubbed his hands together, and leaned toward Octavius. "This clod left a cupboard open in the kitchen when we were putting dishes away. I slammed right into it. Hurts like a sucker."

"You might want to get that looked at," Quincy said.

Mars smiled and nodded awkwardly—*way too awkwardly!*

"Is Suzanne Bartholomew here?" Quincy looked at Octavius for any reaction, then Mars.

"No . . . no, she's not," Octavius said. "She's actually out of town." He stopped there, figuring any more words about location would dig him into a deeper hole.

Quincy nodded. "Who else is in the house right now, if you don't mind me asking?" Again, she examined both of their faces.

The only noise in the house in that instant came from the ticking of the grandfather clock in the dining room.

"Just us," Mars blurted. "Doing some cooking and talking shop."

Octavius wished he hadn't had so much to drink. He'd gotten sloppy. He could sense by her body language and her eyes that Quincy's suspicions were ramping up. And her right hand was now resting on top of her big gun.

"Do either of you know a man who goes by the name Raymond G?" Quincy said.

Octavius and Mars looked at each other and shrugged.

"I don't," Mars said.

Octavius shook his head. "No, can't say that I do."

"Hmm." Quincy took several steps, leaned, and peeked into the large living room.

The instant Octavius heard the furniture bump in the adjacent room, he knew Raymond G had leaned on the chair against the wall that had a slightly uneven leg. Octavius *cursed himself* for not fixing it, and cursed Raymond G for being such a fat klutz.

Quincy's head snapped in the direction of the noise, but in the same motion she rubbed her jaw and slowly looked back into the foyer, trying to act like she hadn't heard it.

Everything flipped to slow motion.

Octavius could tell the wheels in Quincy's head were spinning—her brain was processing what to do next after they'd just told her there was no one else in the house and some bumbling idiot was obviously in the next room.

"Tell you what, gentlemen, I'm not going to take up any more of your evening." Quincy smiled, set her shoulders back, and took a step toward the front door. "I'm sorry to have bothered you." She reached in her coat pocket and handed a white card to Octavius. "If you will, please send me the name and contact info of the person who owns the van as soon as you can."

"Certainly." Octavius took the card with a forced smile, but he knew Quincy was onto them.

He leaned toward her and was on the verge of tackling her right then.

But in one fluid motion Quincy opened the big door and stepped outside as the cold December air filled the foyer. "Goodnight," Quincy said. "Have that cut looked at, mayor."

Mars moved to the door and looked out as it closed. So did Octavius.

"We shouldn't let her go," Octavius whispered, his blood pressure pulsing with each step Quincy took toward her vehicle.

Raymond G entered the foyer and he too stood beside a front window to watch the officer leave.

"We should stop her!" Octavius blurted.

"No," Raymond G said.

"I'm getting the heck out of here," Mars said.

The three men stood in the foyer, each peering out as Quincy approached her car.

"She's going to call for backup," Octavius said. "She heard you in the dining room! She's getting help!"

Mars and Raymond G said nothing because they knew it was true! They could simply walk away and Octavius would be stuck with Timmy's dead body and the women downstairs.

Without a word—because he knew they would tackle him if he said anything—Octavius burst out the front door.

"Officer!" he yelled, reaching behind for his gun as he went down the stone steps. "There's something I forgot to tell you!"

He heard Raymond G whisper loudly, "Get back here!"

But there was no way Octavius was letting Quincy get to her radio.

38

"Here she comes," Wayne said as he and Joanie watched Officer Quincy leave StoneSpell from their car on the street.

"She can't be leaving already." Joanie arched in her seat to see.

Deetz was surprised too, and relieved Quincy hadn't seemed to have found anything amiss inside. She descended the front steps and headed past the van and the mayor's Audi.

"Wait," Joanie said. "Someone's coming out."

Wayne leaned and squinted at the front doors. "Octavius," he said, numbly. "Put your window down—see if we can hear."

They both buzzed their windows down just as Octavius yelled something to Officer Quincy.

The officer had just arrived in front of her patrol car when she turned around to face Octavius.

He was reaching around his back.

"No!" Deetz blurted. "Stay here." He banged his door open, got out, and looked in at Joanie. "Don't leave the car!"

Joanie nodded. "Hurry . . . Be careful!"

Deetz closed the door quietly and moved directly toward the house, quickly jogging down a gravel-filled culvert, and up the other side. He stopped behind several large landscaping rocks just as Octavius raised his gun toward Officer Quincy.

She reached to draw her weapon.

Bam.

A white flash from Octavius's gun.

The first shot missed, the sound of it echoing in Deetz's chest.

Quincy had her gun now and lifted it toward—

Bam!

Another white explosion from Octavius's gun.

Quincy cried out, spun, and dropped to the cobblestone driveway.

Octavius walked toward her slowly, limping.

"You moron! What the heck are you doing?" The white-haired van driver had stepped outside the front door and was screaming at Octavius. Then he disappeared back inside.

Deetz had to help Quincy. He glanced back at Joanie in the SUV, then set his face toward the downed officer and took off toward her.

OCTAVIUS NEVER CLAIMED to be great with a gun. He hardly ever shot one. He missed her the first time and believed he caught the top of the shoulder with the second blast.

The gun had a hellacious kick-back.

He headed toward her to finish the job, his knee aching from when Suzanne had kicked him.

"You stupid *idiot!*" Mars screamed from the steps. "What are you *thinking?* I cannot believe this! Stop!"

The officer was grunting and crawling toward her car.

She was a dead duck.

Suddenly, Raymond G busted out the front doors and went past Mars with the big bag over his shoulder, huffing toward his van.

"Where do you think you're going?" Octavius yelled.

Raymond G opened the back door of the van, threw the bag in, and slammed the door.

"I said, where do you think you're going?" Octavius screamed. "You've got a job to do!"

Raymond G glared at Octavius as he walked fast along the side of the van and opened the driver's door.

Octavius took aim.

"No, don't!" Mars yelled.

Bam.

Octavius's shot exploded the van's side mirror, a foot to the left of Raymond G, whose body jolted and cowered. He clenched his teeth, jumped up into the driver's seat, slammed the door, and the van's engine roared to life.

Octavius cussed, aimed, and fired again.

The shot shattered Raymond G's driver's window, but he was hunched down in the driver's seat. The van thundered and its tires screamed. Raymond G peered low over the dashboard as the van lurched, drifted sideways, finally got traction, and flew out of the driveway. It bounced hard onto the street, sparks flying, and roared into the night.

"Stop this, now!" Mars yelled.

Octavius turned and looked back through the smoke for the cop.

Someone was bent over her!

Wayne Deetz.

Octavius scanned the property but didn't see Deetz's car.

Mars raced back into the house.

Deetz was whispering to Quincy and pulling her toward the doors of the patrol car. He was holding her gun in his right hand.

"Stop!" Octavius yelled.

When they didn't stop, he raised the gun above his head and blasted a shot straight up into the night sky.

Deetz flinched but continued to urge Quincy along toward the car and got the driver's door open.

Octavius was furious now.

His face was on fire.

How dare you!

He lifted the weighty gun again and took aim at Deetz—

Headlights flooded the driveway.

"No!" Deetz screamed and waved frantically at the car that had come out of nowhere. "Go back!"

Octavius made out Joanie's pretty face behind the wheel of the fast-approaching SUV just before its bright lights blinded him and the car rammed him into oblivion.

39

SOME NINETY MINUTES after hearing the 'pops' that sounded like gunshots, Suzanne heard voices and loud noises that she thought were coming from the basement level of StoneSpell.

"Does anyone hear that?" Janine said from her bed in the black room.

"Yes," Suzanne said. "I think I heard gunshots earlier."

"Me, too," came Delia's weak voice from the other side of the room.

"That's the stairs going up," Janine said with alarm in her voice. "Someone's coming."

"It's him!" Delia cried.

Suzanne was stunned by the fear in their voices. She got out of her bed and began crawling toward where she guessed the door was. "I'm going to the door," she said. "Come with me girls. Together we can fight."

Suzanne heard the others get out of their beds.

"I'm over here," Suzanne said. "Show me where the door is."

Janine got to her first. She squeezed Suzanne's arm, took her hand, and led her to the door.

"I'm here," Delia said, finding the other women, embracing them, and squeezing their hands tightly.

"Go for the eyes and the privates," Suzanne whispered, as the locks on the metal door began to open, one by one.

JOANIE SHIVERED and figured she was in a semi state of shock as sirens sounded from all around, and she and Wayne watched the first two ambulances arrive from the front steps of StoneSpell. Paramedics quickly whisked Officer Quincy and Octavius off to the hospital as more and more squad cars and ambulances arrived on the scene, parking at all angles in front of the house.

Amidst the beehive of activity, Joanie was dumbfounded as Mayor Marsden Maddox led Sedona police to the folding staircase in the basement. From there it didn't take them long to discover Octavius's dungeon, where they found Suzanne, Janine, and Delia—very much alive.

Joanie, Wayne, and several officers wrapped the women in blankets in the buzzing living room at StoneSpell, and set out a small smorgasbord of food and beverages for them from Octavius's kitchen while paramedics treated them. They put Suzanne's right shoulder in a temporary sling and cleaned and bandaged the cut on her lip. From police officers' cell phones, the women called their closest family members and, amid sobs and laughter, told them they were alive and urged them to get to Sedona as fast as they could.

Paramedics also tended to the cut on Mayor Maddox's face while he cooperated fully with police, not only leading them to the imprisoned women, but also informing them about the drug operation at DoughWorx and his partnership with Octavius and Timmy.

Crime scene investigators and the county coroner were still in the basement examining Timmy Kondore's body and the scene of his murder. Since Wayne was police, one of the Sedona officers in charge allowed Joanie and him to glimpse at the room in the basement where Octavius kept a wall of surveillance monitors. As she examined the glowing screens with her mouth hanging open, Joanie was speechless, especially when she overheard two technicians speaking softly to each other, and one saying that the two separate monitors off to the side were positioned in Suzanne's apartment. "The guy's dug his own grave," one of them said to the other. "Everything's on here."

A bit later, Joanie and Wayne were told by police that Officer

Quincy was undergoing emergency surgery to remove a bullet from her shoulder and that she was expected to make a full recovery. Octavius was in serious but stable condition and was under strict police supervision at Westside Medical Center, where he was being treated for numerous broken bones, internal bleeding, and a concussion.

A smattering of cheers, laughter, and high-fives went up among police officers at the far corner of the living room. "Your attention!" one of them yelled. "We've successfully apprehended the driver of the van that was here earlier tonight." Officers clapped and hooted. "It turns out he has a long list of aliases and, get this everyone, he's wanted in Nevada for criminal conspiracy and felony murder charges. So, excellent work!"

Joanie and Suzanne sat close to each other on a large ottoman, where Suzanne was wrapped in a blanket, sipping hot cocoa, and had just ended a phone call. She leaned against Joanie and after a few moments of silence she whispered, "I've booked myself into a residential rehab place."

Joanie looked at her caringly and nodded. "That's good. That's what you need right now, isn't it? You just need to get your system cleaned out."

Suzanne nodded and teared up. "It'll take a couple months."

"That's okay." Joanie put an arm around her and brought her close. "You're going to get all better. You're going to be able to start all over."

"I might move back home."

"That might be a good call right now," Joanie said.

"I miss my mom. I'm homesick. I just want to forget the last two years ever happened."

Suzanne leaned her head on Joanie's shoulder.

"We need to stay close now," Joanie said.

Suzanne shook her head. "I'm so sorry about all this." She blurted out a laugh and a cry at the same time. "You weren't expecting this when you came out to visit old Suzanne, were you?"

Joanie laughed, too. "No matter what Wayne and I do, we can never seem to get away from police work—even on vacation!"

"What about that? Have you guys made a decision?" Suzanne

said. "Will he retire now? Or does he want to go back to finish it out?"

Joanie looked across the room at Wayne, who was in a deep discussion with three Sedona Police officers. One of them was taking notes. Perhaps Wayne was giving his statement about what had happened earlier out front with Officer Quincy and Octavius.

"Police work's in his blood," Joanie said. "I'm not sure he's quite ready to give it up. I'm trying to leave it up to him. If it were up to me he'd have been done a year ago."

"You should be proud of your marriage, Joanie. How long's it been?"

"Thirty-four years."

They sat in silence for a moment.

Joanie felt sorry for Suzanne, because the man she'd fallen in love with was a selfish, hurtful, sinister liar—nothing more than a charm artist.

Suzanne looked at the time on her phone. "Do you think you guys could take me to my place?" she said. "I can't check into the rehab until tomorrow at ten."

"Sure. Will you be okay?" Joanie said. "If you want, you can stay with us tonight. We can take you to the place in the morning."

Suzanne looked away, out the window, into the blackness.

Then she dropped her head and her shoulders bounced ever so slightly.

She was crying.

Joanie put an arm around her again. "You're going to make it, Suzanne. I know you are."

With her head still down, Suzanne nodded and whispered, "With God's help . . . only with God's help."

WHAT'S NEXT FROM CRESTON?

If you're ready to continue the remarkable story of Wayne Deetz and his beloved family, check out book five in the Signs of Life Series on **Amazon**:

ABOUT THE AUTHOR

Creston Mapes grew up in northeast Ohio, where he has fond memories of living with his family of five in the upstairs portion of his dad's early American furniture store - The Weathervane Shop. Creston was not a good student, but the one natural talent he possessed was writing.

He set type by hand and cranked out his own neighborhood newspaper as a kid, then went on to graduate with a degree in journalism from Bowling Green State University. Creston was a newspaper reporter and photographer in Ohio and Florida, then moved to Atlanta, Georgia, for a job as a creative copywriter.

Creston served for a stint as a creative director, but quickly learned he was not cut out for management. He went out on his own as a freelance writer in 1991 and, over the next 30 years, did work for Chick-fil-A, Coca-Cola, The Weather Channel, Oracle, ABC-TV, TNT Sports, colleges and universities, ad agencies, and more. He's ghost-written more than ten non-fiction books.

Along the way, Creston has written many contemporary thrillers, achieved Amazon Bestseller status multiple times, and had one of his novels (*Nobody*) optioned as a major motion picture.

Creston married his fourth-grade sweetheart, Patty, and they have four amazing adult children. Creston loves his part-time job as an usher at local venues where he gets to see all the latest-greatest concerts and sporting events. He enjoys reading, fishing, thrifting, time with his family, and dates with his wife.

To keep informed of special deals, giveaways, new releases, and exclusive updates from Creston, sign up for his newsletter at: **CrestonMapes.com/contact**

To view all of Creston's eBooks, audiobooks, and paperbacks go to **Amazon.com/author/crestonmapes**

STAND ALONE THRILLERS
I Am In Here
Nobody

SIGNS OF LIFE SERIES
Signs of Life
Let My Daughter Go
I Pick You
Charm Artist
Son & Shield
Secrets in Shadows

THE CRITTENDON FILES
Fear Has a Name
Poison Town
Sky Zone

ROCK STAR CHRONICLES
Dark Star: Confessions of a Rock Idol
Full Tilt

www.ingramcontent.com/pod-product-compliance
Lightning Source LLC
LaVergne TN
LVHW021235080526
838199LV00088B/4517